Protecting Caroline

Protecting Caroline

SEAL of Protection
Book 1

By Susan Stoker

Table of Contents

Acknowledgements

I would like to take the time to thank my awesome editor, Missy B., for polishing up my words and making Wolf and Caroline's story even better.

To my wonderful Stoker Aces...ya'll are the best street team ever. We might not be big, but you guys do such a great job in supporting me and pimping me out! Thank you!

To Connie N—Thank you for being my very first Beta reader for Protecting Caroline and giving me GREAT tips that I think helped make the story so much better.

To Amy H—Wow, you gave me the confidence I needed to really work to get this series out. Thank you for all your encouragement and tips, every day. It means more than you'll know.

To my friends and family, who I am sure are wondering when I'm going to be "over this writing thing"...thanks for putting up with me!

To all my readers, thank you for taking a chance on me. Without you I'm not sure I'd be putting my stories out there.

Prologue

MATTHEW "WOLF" STEEL couldn't be more proud of his five teammates, and friends. SEAL teams were notoriously tight, and his team was no different. The SEALs were exhausted. They'd just spent the last two weeks at an "undisclosed location" trying to ferret out the head bad guy in a nest of hundreds of other bad guys. It'd been a hell of mission, but one they'd ultimately succeeded in accomplishing.

Looking around the plane, Wolf observed the sleeping men. He really should be crashed as they were, but he still had way too much adrenaline coursing through his body to relax just yet. He knew he'd be out for the count later, but for now, he was wide awake.

Christopher "Abe" Powers was the first to catch Wolf's eye. Abe was probably his closest friend of the group. Wolf thought he was the only one of the group who knew even a little bit of Abe's background, but it was uncanny how well the nickname fit Abe. The man was as honest as the day was long and Abe demanded that same honesty in those he called his friends.

Wolf watched as Abe shifted in his seat and then settled once again. Wolf then looked over to Hunter "Cookie" Knox. Cookie had been the most recent addition to their team, but no one looked down on him as a result. Unlike many businesses, it didn't matter if a SEAL was fresh out of Seal Qualification Training or had been on a team for years, a SEAL is a SEAL.

The group was still getting to know Cookie, but he'd proven to be a great addition to their close-knit team. Cookie was the best swimmer out of all of them; he was funny, compassionate, and never hesitated to do whatever it took to get the job done.

Faulkner "Dude" Cooper's mutterings drew Wolf's attention. Dude hadn't taken any of his gear off and was sitting scrunched into the little seat on the military plane. Wolf remembered when Dude was almost blown up trying to secure a building. As their resident explosives expert, Dude found a booby trapped M14 mine duct taped to a door jamb during one of their missions. The mine was nicknamed "toe popper" because it was designed to maim and slow down people entering a room, rather than kill them.

Dude had immediately recognized the type of mine and had moved to re-insert the safety clip to disarm it, but something had gone wrong and the bomb went off. The mine did what it was intended to do; resulting in

Dude losing parts of three of his fingers on his left hand. He had extensive scarring as well as missing parts of his hand as a consequence of being too close to the mine when it exploded.

Wolf knew Dude was more sensitive about his injury than he'd ever let on to any of his teammates. Wolf had seen Dude's face go blank and cold when a woman rejected him after seeing his mangled hand. Although he missed his friend's happy-go-lucky attitude at times, Wolf was thankful Dude was still with them. With the best instincts when it came to explosives, Wolf knew the team was better off because Dude was on it.

Thinking about Dude's issues with women caused Wolf to reflect upon Sam "Mozart" Reed. That was one man who certainly didn't have any problems with women. Mozart was popular with the ladies and never hesitated to turn any encounter into one which involved flirting and the possibility of a one-night-stand. As far as Wolf knew, however, Mozart had never been tempted into anything more.

Wolf figured Mozart's aversion to settling down with one woman had something to do with Mozart's little sister being murdered when he was a child, but Wolf never pried. A man was allowed to have his secrets.

Wolf chuckled to himself thinking about the last man on their team, Kason "Benny" Sawyer. Nicknames were a part of life on SEAL teams. Everyone got one and it wasn't necessarily something that was macho or even wanted by the recipient. Benny was a case in point. He'd been trying for years to get the guys to change his name, but they'd just laughed and ignored him. An inside joke with the team, they'd ask Benny if he liked some new name only to just laugh and say "too bad" when Benny agreed that he loved the new one. Benny had earned his nickname fair and square, and nothing he could say would change it.

Feeling tired for the first time since he'd climbed onto the plane, Wolf finally closed his eyes. He felt lucky he not only had one of the most interesting and exciting jobs in the world, but that he was able to work with such a great group of men. Each man had his strengths and weaknesses and there were no secrets within the group. Abe, Cookie, Mozart, Benny, and Dude were teammates, but they were also his closest friends.

Wolf sighed, settled himself into his seat and tried to get comfortable. The team would most likely have a few weeks stateside before being sent on another mission, but time off was never guaranteed. Wolf knew the night after they returned, the team would head to their favorite bar for a "post-mission" ritual of blowing off steam and shooting the shit.

Leaving the mission behind was sometimes difficult, but somehow their tradition of throwing back a few beers would break the team out of the military frame of mind and bring them back to what was important...friendship and women.

Wolf figured each team member knew they most likely wouldn't meet the woman of their dreams in a bar—especially not in a bar near the base where too many women were more than willing to sleep with a SEAL just to say she'd done it. But, it didn't stop the boys from enjoying what was frequently offered.

Wolf ignored the niggling little voice in his head that said he wouldn't mind settling down and finding someone to love. It wasn't as if he could plan it, he'd just have to go with the flow. Hopefully it happened sooner rather than later, but he wasn't going to act desperate about it.

Sleep finally came over Wolf, as it had the rest of his team, and they all slept the sleep of the exhausted as they flew toward California, and home.

Chapter One

LIKE A FANTASY brought to life, each woman in the bar was acutely aware of the table full of gorgeous men sitting in the corner. Obviously in the military, they were muscular and had a wariness about them that came from too many missions overseas. Every one of the women would have given anything to be able to go home with one of them—they were *that* good looking.

The group of six teammates and friends were enjoying a final beer together before some of them headed off on leave. Known for its excellent beer choices and as a good place to pick up women, the bar was where they spent quite a bit of time, especially after a mission. All six men had gone home with a woman they'd met there at one time or another. So far none of them had found "the one." It wasn't as if they didn't *want* to find someone to love, it just hadn't happened for any of them yet, and in the meantime they all enjoyed playing the field.

All of the men had played the pick-up game at one

time or another, but Wolf was the least likely to hook up with a random chick who just wanted to bag a SEAL. He'd learned at a young age, by looking at the example his folks set, that true love was out there and could be found. Wolf wasn't a saint, but he also never flaunted his sexuality.

"You ready for your vacation?" Dude asked Wolf.

"Oh, hell yeah! I can't remember the last time I took some time off…hell, when *any* of us took time off."

"Where are you guys going again?" Dude questioned.

"Mozart, Abe, and I are headed out to Virginia to visit Tex. We've been using him on more and more missions lately because he's got some amazing contacts the Navy couldn't hope to replicate."

Taking a breath, Wolf continued, "After Tex lost his leg on that mission, he retired and it's been way too long since we've seen him. Since we're slated to leave out of Norfolk in a couple of weeks for our next mission, we thought we'd take some R&R and head out there beforehand."

Everyone around the table nodded at Wolf's explanation of where he, Abe and Mozart were going in Virginia. Benny, Dude, and Cookie also knew Tex well and were glad Wolf and the others would get to spend some time with him.

"That sucks he left the Navy," Benny said, "but I get

it. If I couldn't stay with you guys and a team, I wouldn't want to stay in only to have to work a desk."

"Yeah, but can you imagine how much harder some of the shit we do would be if it wasn't for him?" Mozart responded. "Seriously, I have no idea how Tex gets the information he does, but I don't think we'd be as quick to get through some of our missions without him."

"Yeah, he seriously is scary with that computer shit," Cookie enthused. "Tex can find anyone, no matter where they are."

Mozart nodded. "I certainly hope that's true. He's working on something personal for me and I really need him to come through."

Wolf thumped Mozart on his back. "I'm sure he will. Given enough time Tex always comes through. Hey, you ready for Norfolk?"

Mozart's mood lifted immediately at Wolf's question. "Can't wait! Heard there are some awesome bars around the base out there and not as many SEALs to compete for the ladies."

Everyone laughed. The group knew how much Mozart loved finding "fresh meat" to convince to go back to his room with him.

The men sat in the bar until late in the evening, talking and enjoying their time together. Typically the conversation would veer toward women, alcohol, and their job. Because Wolf, Abe, and Mozart had get to the airport early in the morning, they eased off their typical competitive natures about who could drink the most and spent their time relaxing and playing the odd game of pool.

Finally, as the evening turned into night and the crowd began to get thicker and more uninhibited, Abe thunked his empty bottle on the table and sighed, "Damn, wish we weren't leaving so early in the morning, that chick at the bar's been checking me out all night."

Cookie laughed. "As much as I hate to agree with you, especially considering it makes me sound too much like Mozart, I think you're right. And if I'm not mistaken, her friend's been checking *me* out."

Everyone laughed because they'd noticed the duo at the bar making eyes at them all night. It was obvious the women didn't really care who they ended up with, as long as they went home with a SEAL, but their eyes followed Cookie and Abe more than the others.

"The one on the right is Adelaide and the one on the left is Michele," Mozart told them knowingly.

Wolf just raised an eyebrow at his teammate while everyone else demanded to know how Mozart knew who the women were.

"They come here all the time. I *might* have gotten to know them both reaaally well a couple of weeks ago. I'm sure they'll be willing to get to know you better when you get back, Abe."

Nobody was surprised at Mozart's words. Taking on two women at a time was just the type of thing they'd expect out of him. None of them doubted that Mozart was telling the truth and not just bragging. The group knew him too well.

"I'm a one-woman-at-a-time man," Abe told the group laughing. "But Adelaide looks like my kind of woman. I think I'll see if she might be interested in a few weeks when we get back home."

Everyone knew he was warning them off. Abe didn't stand for poaching. The men chuckled at his claim, used to Abe's quirks when it came to women.

"As much fun as this has been, I'm gonna hit the road," Wolf announced to the group, not in the least abashed to be the first person leaving for the night.

"Yeah, me too," Mozart chimed in.

"We'll see the rest of you guys in a couple weeks in Norfolk," Abe told his friends and teammates as he stood up, joining Wolf and Mozart as they got ready to leave.

The three men smacked each other on the back good-naturedly as they said their good-byes to the rest of the group and headed out the door, disappearing into the night.

Cookie, Benny, and Dude pushed back their chairs not too much later to leave as well. "See you guys in the morning at PT," Dude told them as they walked out through the door of the bar.

"You'd think with the others gone we'd at least get a morning off from training," Cookie mock grumbled. Benny and Dude laughed, knowing Cookie loved to work out, never missing PT unless he was sick or recovering from an injury.

"Whatever Cookie, you know the CO has a ten miler scheduled. You'll be there before all of us."

Cookie just laughed. The men gave chin lifts to each other and faded into the parking lot to their cars and into the night.

A previous commander of the SEAL team once remarked to an Officer that had been visiting the base that this group of six men were one of the best teams he'd ever commanded, not because of the skills they'd learned during Hell Week or because of their strength, but because of the genuine respect they had for each other.

"Those men would do anything for each other. They're the epitome of the word "team." If ever I needed rescuing or protecting, those would be the men I'd want."

Chapter Two

CAROLINE SHIFTED UNCOMFORTABLY in her seat. She hated flying. She hadn't flown much and there were just too many people, too close together. She tried to ignore the people walking down the aisle to their seats. At least she'd gotten an aisle seat close to the front of the plane. Caroline watched the shoes of the people passing her. She felt too awkward to look into people's eyes as they lumbered past. The boarding process was one of the parts of flying Caroline hated the most…waiting to see who'd be in the seat next to her. Looking out the corner of her eye at the man sitting in the window seat, she noticed he was already settled in, reading a newspaper; not paying any attention to the rest of the passengers as they shuffled by their row.

Sneakers, flip flops, sneakers, loafers, sandals, boots….the boots didn't pass. She looked up and saw a man had stopped next to her seat.

"I guess I'm in the middle then," he said in a deep voice that sent shivers straight through her.

Caroline nodded and stood up to let him pass. Brushing against her as he moved past, he settled himself into the seat next to her. The dreaded middle seat. The man wasn't overweight, far from it, but he certainly wasn't small. It was a cozy fit. Caroline's shoulders literally rubbed against his when she sat back down—she wouldn't be using the armrest for the flight.

He was one hell of a man that was sure. He was tall, when she'd stood up to let him into the row she'd barely came to his shoulder. And holy hell, he was muscular. She wondered for a moment if he was a body builder. If she wrapped both hands around his bicep, Caroline didn't think her hands would touch. The man was wearing long sleeves, but she could see the fabric straining over his biceps. He was sporting a pair of cargo pants, the kind with the multitude of pockets. As they sat, Caroline could see his legs were just as muscular as the rest of him. She blushed a bit and tore her eyes away. Woah. He could be a model and would probably make a killing. She knew he probably wasn't though. He was too rugged, too masculine, too...well...manly to be any kind of model, no matter what he'd make doing it.

The man next to her shifted a bit and laid his head back on the head rest and closed his eyes.

Caroline fought with her conscience. She hated the middle seat. She really did, but there was no way this man would last the entire four hour flight squished in between her and the other man the way he was. With his knees hitting the chair in front of him, he looked scrunched. His muscular body sure didn't leave any extra room in the small cramped airline seat. He looked miserable. Caroline sighed, knowing what she had to do.

WOLF SAT UNCOMFORTABLY in the airplane seat. Outwardly he looked relaxed, but he was anything but. With eyes closed, Wolf processed the sounds around him. The passengers walking past his row to their seats, the sounds of the overhead bins filling up, the rustle of the newspaper from the man to his right, and the quiet sigh of the woman sitting to his left.

Flying commercial from San Diego to the base in Norfolk, Wolf, Mozart, and Abe were technically off duty at the moment, and were flying in civilian clothes. They'd booked this flight last minute, thus leaving him the middle seat and the others spread out in the plane. Wolf wanted to hop on a MAC flight, the free flight service offered by the military to members and spouses, but he knew there was no guarantee they'd get a space on the flight and the three of them wanted to get to Virginia to see Tex sooner rather than later. They talked to Tex all the time since he helped them get information when they needed it, but talking to him in an official capacity was way different than being able to sit down around a table, drink a beer, and talk about anything other than work.

Wolf, Abe, and Mozart were supposed to be on leave before their next mission started. They were leaving from Norfolk in two weeks, and the thought of being able to shut down and actually enjoy being around friends was a welcome one. They all spent way too much time hyped up and in danger. Spending two weeks before they had to risk their lives on another mission was just too tempting to turn down.

None of them had a lot of time off recently and Wolf, Abe, and Mozart were happy to get to pretend to be normal for a few weeks before they had to leave again. Wolf had been a SEAL for ten years, working with Mozart and Abe for the last eight. They hadn't been in BUD/S together, but that didn't matter. Bonded over firefights, scuba dives, and life threatening situations, they'd each saved each other's lives a few times and their connection was tighter than most siblings.

Wolf would've preferred to sit in the same row with his friends, but because they'd made their flight arrangements so late, they didn't have a choice and had to take seats that were available. Mozart offered to flirt with the airline employee in the hopes they'd be able to get upgraded, or at least be seated together, but they'd agreed to suck it up and sit where they were assigned. They all knew they wouldn't fit in the seats if they all sat in the same row anyway. Their shoulders were just too broad to fit comfortably side-by-side in a crunched airline row. Wolf knew his friends felt the same way he did—they didn't flaunt their SEAL status to receive preferential treatment. It was bad enough women hit on them back home in San Diego in the bars just because they were SEALs.

Wolf hated to admit it, but he'd gotten bored with the bar scene. He was picky in the first place, and he'd found too many women just wanted to sleep with a SEAL, it didn't matter *who* the SEAL was, just that they could brag later to their friends they'd done it with a legendary SEAL. The sadder part was that too many SEALs took advantage of it. Wolf could admit to himself that once upon a time he'd done that exact thing, but time and experience had shown him the encounters left him feeling dissatisfied and used. If someone had asked him right after he'd graduated from BUD/S if he'd ever feel used by a woman who wanted to sleep with him, he would've laughed himself silly.

Wolf knew what love looked like. His parents had been together for almost forty years. They were still as madly in love now as they were when they got married. It used to embarrass him, but lately it made him feel wistful. They'd still go on dates and hold hands wherever they went. His dad surprised his mom with romantic gifts and, every now and then, a special trip. Wolf wanted what his parents had. He wanted someone he could be himself with. He wanted someone to need him. He wanted to need someone. Wolf supposed it wasn't manly to admit any of those things, but it was what it was.

Wolf had no idea how to go about finding that special woman though, except he knew he wouldn't find her in a bar. The other issue was that he was a SEAL. He was sent off to crappy little countries to kill people and to keep the peace. Every now and then they were sent off on a rescue mission. He wasn't allowed to talk about the specifics of what he did with anyone. He had no idea how that would work in a marriage. He'd seen too many of his SEAL friends get married and then divorced because their wives just couldn't handle the secrecy and the uncertainty of when their husbands would be coming home, or even where they were going in the first place.

To be fair, not all of the marriages ended because of the secrecy and danger inherent in being a SEAL. Some ended because one of the people in the marriage cheated on the other. Sometimes it was the wife who cheated, and other times it was the husband. Wolf shrugged. There wasn't any use in obsessing about it. Hopefully he'd someday find someone to settle down with. If it didn't happen during his military career, perhaps it would once he was retired. There was no rule that said someone in their forties couldn't find true love and get married.

After drifting off and thinking about his lack of a love life, Wolf flinched when he felt a hand on his arm. He hadn't been paying attention and was actually startled. His team would get a kick out of that. Wolf was known to always be one step ahead of the enemy and to be able to have a good idea what they were going do before they did it. Now here he was letting a civilian take him by surprise.

He opened his eyes to look at the woman sitting in the aisle seat next to him. She was ordinary. He took in her jeans, sneakers, and long sleeve T-shirt at a glance. Her brown hair was pulled up into a messy knot at the back of her head. She looked to be in her early thirties. She wore no rings; had very little makeup on, her nails weren't polished; she had little gold studs in each ear and was looking at him expectantly. He inwardly sighed. When he was younger Wolf loved when women hit on him, now it had gotten old. Granted, this woman didn't look like she was the type to throw herself at a man, but he'd learned that looks were deceiving when it came to what women wanted.

Glancing in her direction, Wolf thought the woman appeared to be mulling over telling him something. This in itself was fascinating, since in his experience, women tended to get right to the point of what they wanted to say. Her hesitation made him more interested in hearing what she had to say to him and he waited, patiently, as she gathered her thoughts.

Chapter Three

C AROLINE WAS NERVOUS. She wanted to talk to the over-the-top masculine man sitting next to her, but she didn't want him to look through her as most men did. Caroline had faded into the woodwork most of her life. No boyfriend in high school, she hadn't gone to any of the school dances, not even prom.

One guy had the nerve to tell her that she wasn't "girlfriend material." Thinking back to that comment, made without thought, still hurt her today. Caroline knew she wasn't model beautiful, but she didn't think she was a troll either. She wasn't tall like men seemed to want in a woman, but she wasn't short and cute either. Caroline was average from the top of her brown-haired head to the bottom of her normal sized feet.

She'd always been the "friend" growing up. All the boys liked to talk to her, but only to get Caroline's opinion on the other girls and if they liked them. It was depressing as hell, but she'd gotten used to it. When she got old enough to really care and actually want to go to dances and dates, Caroline was firmly in the "friend" category and she'd sat at home while everyone else went out and had a good time.

The media's portrayals of the "perfect woman" didn't only affect women and girls, but it did the same with men. Men all seemed to want the skinny, perky, bubbly, woman they'd seen on television and in magazines all their lives. From reality shows to news casters and even to sit-coms, today's world was bombarded with flawless women, beautiful from sun-up to sundown.

That just wasn't Caroline. She wasn't a genius, but she also wasn't dumb. She worked hard at her job and did her part to make the world go-'round. But she often wished, when she was lying in bed late at night, that she could find a man that would *see* her. See the real her.

Caroline's parents had her late in their life, and had recently passed away. She missed them. They'd been her staunchest supporters. Whatever she wanted to do, they'd encouraged her and told her she could do it. Without her parents and no close friends to keep her there, California didn't have the appeal to Caroline that it used to.

Caroline thought about the man sitting next to her. He probably had a lot of close friends. He looked trustworthy. Caroline almost snorted at her own thoughts. How the hell could someone "look" trustworthy? It was ridiculous. Didn't all the crime shows talk about how the killer always looked like the "guy next door?"

Caroline shook herself. She had to stop her line of thought or she'd depress herself even more than she already was. Who cared if this guy didn't "see" her? She'd only be sitting next to him for a couple of hours, and then they'd go their separate ways once they landed in Virginia. Hell, she knew he didn't really take note of her. He'd already met her, and when he'd sat down he'd looked right through her as if he'd never seen her before. It happened to her all the time, over and over. She should be used to it, but it seemed to hurt more this time.

Caroline had hesitated to touch him. She didn't really want to disturb the man, but it wasn't in her nature to let him suffer in that middle seat. Because he certainly was suffering. He looked jammed into the seat. Caroline knew he'd be stiff and uncomfortable by the time they landed in Virginia if he sat there the entire flight.

Caroline jerked her hand away after he flinched. She didn't mean to startle him, and for a second thought that if he decided he wanted to strike out at her, he could really hurt her. Not that she thought he would, but anyone that reacted that quickly and suddenly certainly wasn't used to being surprised.

Now he was looking at her expectantly. She'd gotten

his attention and Caroline needed to follow through. She steeled herself and gave herself a quick pep talk. She just had to say it quickly before she lost her nerve.

"Um…Do you want to switch seats?"

He didn't answer, but raised his eyebrows as if to ask why she was offering.

Geez, even his eyebrow lift was sexy. "You don't look comfortable," Caroline told him bluntly and honestly. "I'll switch with you, that way you can at least have a little bit more leg room here in the aisle."

Wolf stared at the woman. Why was she offering? He wasn't sure, but he wasn't an idiot, he wasn't going to turn down her offer. He was miserable. If she made a move on him later in the flight he'd just have to politely rebuff her. Jesus, he was cocky and conceited. He decided to think that the nondescript woman sitting next to simply wanted to do something nice for a stranger. He'd believe that until he was proved wrong. If he *was* proven wrong, he'd figure out a game plan then. Arriving at his decision, he nodded once and told her simply, "Thanks."

Standing up and allowing the man to move out of the row, Caroline scooted past him and into the middle seat. There was something very intimate about sitting in the seat while it was still warm from his body. Especially when she thought about *what* body part had just been there. Caroline tried to put that out of her mind.

Sheesh. *Get your mind out of the gutter!* Caroline admonished herself.

Caroline knew he didn't need her slobbering all over him. She figured he had women throwing themselves at him all the time. After throwing out the "body builder" thought she'd had earlier, she guessed he was probably in the military. She hadn't met one "normal" man who looked like him who wasn't in the military. Especially considering they were flying from San Diego, home of the one of the biggest Naval bases in the United States.

When the man leaned down to grab his backpack he'd stowed under the middle seat, Caroline stopped him.

"It's okay, just leave it. It'll give you more room for your legs."

"Are you sure?"

"Of course. Your bag isn't even really blocking my legs at all, I'm short." She chuckled at herself.

Chapter Four

W OLF LOOKED MORE closely at the woman as he got comfortable and buckled his seat belt in the aisle seat. He was grateful for the extra room she'd just granted him by allowing him to leave his bag at her feet, but he didn't understand why she'd do it.

The woman turned away from Wolf to buckle her seatbelt. It didn't seem like she was trying to flirt with him or to get him to notice her. But the fact that she wasn't, only seemed to draw his attention to her more. Maybe that was her plan all along?

Wolf wasn't a man who was used to unselfish acts by other people. He lived in a world where people were deceitful and underhanded and would do anything they could to get ahead. Hell, in certain parts of the world they'd even kill someone if it meant more power, more money, or even more food to eat. Granted, giving up a comfortable seat on a plane wasn't even in the same league as what Wolf had seen people do to gain an advantage, but that was what made it so unusual.

Caroline could feel the man's eyes on her. It discomfited her. Shifting uneasily in her seat, Caroline wasn't used to men looking at her that closely. She was plain and uninteresting. She knew it and so did everyone else. Caroline wasn't the type of person who got special favors because of her looks, and she wasn't one to draw the attention of any man. She'd long ago learned to accept it. Caroline had a pretty healthy self-esteem, even with her plain looks. She'd had a tough time growing up, what teenaged girl didn't, but when all was said and done, Caroline learned to actually like herself. She was smart, had a good personality, and even if she didn't have men lining up to take her out, she was mostly content with herself and her life.

Thinking about her childhood and her parents made Caroline smile. Her mom and dad always encouraged her to be who she was. Remembering when she told her dad what she wanted to do after she graduated from high school, Caroline's smile grew wider. Some dads would've been disappointed, but not hers. All he'd done was kiss her on the forehead and say, "You can do anything you want to do Caroline. You're the smartest woman I know and I'm very proud of you." Caroline held that memory close to her heart and drew on it when she was feeling down.

Caroline snuck a peek at the man who was now sitting in the aisle seat and blushed, yup, he was still watching her.

Wolf watched as the woman glanced at him and then blushed furiously seeing his eyes on her. When was the last time he'd seen a woman blush? He couldn't remember. It was past time they introduced themselves. He held out his hand to her. "Matthew," he said softly. Wolf hadn't been around a lot of people who didn't have any connections to the military. He usually used his nickname when introducing himself, it was such an ingrained part of him, but he didn't want to freak this woman out. Wolf wasn't exactly a normal name for someone to call themselves in the civilian world.

Hoping she'd reciprocate and shake his hand, he waited for her to give him her hand. Wolf learned a lot about people by their handshake. Many women felt as if they shouldn't squeeze a man's hand when they met, so they just let their hand lay limply in his as they shook. He hated that. Wolf had no idea where that had come from, but if women knew how much it turned men off, they'd certainly stop doing it.

Caroline tentatively took his hand, but shook it with strength. She hoped he didn't squeeze her hand too hard in an effort to show off how strong he was. He could easily crush her fingers. She'd had that happen in the past too, especially since she worked with a lot of men. They'd exert what they thought was dominance, by clenching her hand too tight. It didn't exude dominance, only assholed-ness.

"Caroline," she reciprocated softly.

Wolf squeezed her hand and was pleasantly surprised at the softness interspersed with calluses on her palm. She obviously wasn't one to sit around; she worked with her hands in some way.

Of course thinking about the texture of her palm immediately made him think about how it'd feel caressing his body. Wolf was immediately ashamed of himself. Jesus, it'd obviously been way too long since he'd been with a woman if a simple handshake made him hard. He shifted in his seat trying to hide his arousal from the slight woman innocently sitting next to him.

Caroline was also pleased at their handshake. The man didn't squeeze her fingers too hard, and seemed to lighten up a bit after they dropped their hands. She noticed he shifted restlessly, but figured he was just trying to get comfortable in the cramped airplane seat.

They smiled at each other before directing their attention to the flight attendant at the front of the plane.

Another flight attendant came over the speaker and asked that all electronic devices be turned off, or put in airplane mode, and to prepare for takeoff.

Caroline watched as the attendant in the aisle went through the motions of showing the passengers how to put on their seatbelt, how to use the lifejacket in case of a water landing, and how to operate the flimsy oxygen thingies that would fall from the ceiling of the plane in case of depressurization. Caroline didn't want to think of the panic that would ensue in the plane if any of those things actually happened.

Caroline noticed that the flight attendant seemed extra bored. She figured giving the same demonstration to a plane full of people who were ignoring you could get old really fast, but wasn't it their job to at least *pretend* to have enthusiasm while doing it? She'd seen the video clips online of flight attendants who joked and danced, she'd never been on a flight with one who had done that, but these guys actually looked annoyed and uninterested about the entire pre-flight routine. It was weird.

Caroline mentally shrugged, it wasn't as if she could do anything about it, and turned her attention to the *SkyMall* magazine in the seat pocket in front of her. She idly flipped the pages, looking at the overpriced items as the plane taxied to the runway and took off.

After safely reaching cruising altitude, Caroline put the magazine back into the pocket in front of her and rested her head on the seatback, much as Matthew had done when he'd first sat down. She was tired, but the middle seat wasn't conducive to sleeping with nothing to rest her head against and there was no way she'd risk falling asleep with her head tilted back on the seat. She'd probably snore like an eighty year old man if she did. Even if the sexy man next to her wasn't interested, she still didn't want to embarrass herself. She had *some* standards after all.

Caroline looked over at Matthew and saw he also wasn't sleeping. He had one leg stretched out into the aisle and one under the seat in front of him. His eyes were closed and his hands were intertwined, resting on his stomach. Every now and then he'd shift in his seat, open his eyes, and close them again. She smiled. At least in the aisle seat he was more comfortable than if he'd been scrunched in the middle.

Wolf opened his eyes with a sigh; there was no way he was sleeping. Airplane seats sucked, another reason not to fly commercial. Not knowing why he couldn't keep his eyes off of her, Wolf glanced over at the woman sitting next to him again, and caught Caroline's smile which lit up her whole face. Wolf thought that while she wasn't conventionally pretty, she was certainly interesting looking.

"So, you come here often?" He couldn't resist the cheesy pickup line. Something told him Caroline would think it was funny and not take him seriously. Hearing her soft laugh, Wolf knew he was right.

"Ha-ha. Actually, I don't fly too often, but I'm currently on my way to a new job in Norfolk. Normally I'd drive, but my new company is paying all my moving expenses, including shipping my car out to Virginia, so I figured instead of taking the extra days to drive cross country, I'd just fly and take the extra time to get to know Norfolk before I have to start work."

"Sounds sensible." Wolf agreed, happy to hear she seemed like a reasonable woman. He'd met too many women that were all about the money, or fame, or fashion, or whatever.

"What are you doing in Norfolk? Or is that just a stop-over to somewhere else?" Caroline asked curiously. She wasn't trying to pry, but since he was talking to her and seemed interested in what she had to say, she wanted to keep the conversation going.

Wolf knew he had to be careful about talking about his job, but he figured since they weren't on their way to a mission right now he could be mostly upfront. "I and two buddies are headed for some leave in Virginia. We're between missions...er...jobs right now."

"I figured you were military." Caroline told him matter-of-factly with no surprise or awe in her voice.

"How'd you guess?"

Caroline couldn't tell if he was being serious or just kidding with her. "I don't know if that was sarcasm or not, but I noticed you're very much in shape, you have combat boots on, and honestly, you just have the look of a military man."

Wolf laughed. "I was teasing you Caroline, but yeah,

you're right. I'm in the Navy. I'm a SEAL." Wolf was surprised at himself. He didn't usually blurt out that he was a SEAL. There was something about this woman that invited confidences. He wasn't sure what to expect from her with his revelation, but was honestly surprised when she didn't say anything about it and continued their conversation as if Wolf never mentioned he was a member of one of the most revered and respected branches of their country's military.

"What are you going to do on your leave?"

"We have a friend who lives out there. He was medically retired after losing a leg in combat. We're just going to crash at his house and hang out. We'll probably go to the base and check it out, but we all decided we needed the down time and try to keep the shop talk to a minimum."

"Oh geez, that sucks about your friend. I'm so sorry. I'm so glad people today recognize what you guys do for our country. I knew someone in high school that told me when her dad came home from Vietnam he was spit on and generally treated like crap. It's such a shame and I love seeing the support all our country's soldiers get today. I think it's a good idea for you and your friends to take some time off and for you to try to keep talk about your job out of it," Caroline agreed. "It can be tough to really relax if all you do on a vacation is talk shop."

Enjoying the conversation more than he'd thought he would, Wolf asked, "So, what is this new job you're flying across the country for?"

Pleased he was showing interest in her, Caroline told him, hoping it wouldn't turn him off—some men didn't like smart women. "I'm a chemist. I decided I needed a change of scenery since my parents passed away. I researched where I wanted to work and applied for, and was hired, by a great company out east. I'm pretty excited to get started actually."

"So what does a chemist do exactly?" Wolf was impressed with what he'd heard so far.

Caroline laughed lightly. She wasn't exactly surprised at the question. It seemed like most people had no idea what she did most of the time, even when she explained it she could see their eyes glaze over. Well, he'd asked, so she decided to tell him. She was enjoying talking to him and he seemed pretty smart. She had high hopes he'd understand.

"There are two basic 'worlds' when it comes to chemists. A macroscopic world in chemistry is the one that you'd probably think of when thinking of a chemist. It involves a lab and white coats and experimenting with different compounds and materials. You can actually see, hear, and touch things in the macroscopic world. On the other hand is the microscopic world. This involves things you can't actually touch or hear or see. It basically deals with models and theories mostly."

"Which do you work in?" Wolf asked, seemingly following her conversation without any issues.

"I'm a card carrying, lab coat wearing, chemist geek," Caroline answered laughing at herself.

Wolf didn't think, but reached over and took her hand in his. "You're not a geek sweetheart; you're a scholar in a lab coat who does magic with her hands."

Holy crap. This man was lethal. Caroline's stomach clenched at his words. Had any man, ever, said anything nicer to her than that? She didn't think so. She tried to blow off his words and airily joked, "Actually I have a wand that does the magic."

"Tell me more about your job. It sounds really interesting." Sensing Caroline's reluctance, Wolf begged, "Please?"

Embarrassed, but not sure why, Caroline hesitantly told him more. "I'm in applied chemistry; I work for a company and do short term research on whatever is on my plate at the time. It could be product development or improvement to something that's already out there. There are also pure chemists who do more long term research on whatever they want or can get funded and there's no real practical application in the short term with them."

"So what do you do all day at work?" Wolf found Caroline fascinating. He'd never met a chemist before.

Oh sure, Wolf met people who were good at chemistry and had a knack for things like making bombs for the military, as well as defusing them, like Dude. But being a bomb ordinance technician wasn't the same thing as being a chemist. It wasn't like Wolf came in contact with someone like Caroline in his regular world.

"Well, it depends on the day and the project, of course," she told him, losing her self-consciousness since she was talking about a topic she loved. Caroline had no idea her enthusiasm made her prettier and that Wolf thought her excitement was a turn on.

"Sometimes I analyze substances, trying to figure out what's in it, how much of something is in it, or both. I can create substances too. Sometimes we make synthetic substances, trying to copy something that's in nature, and other times we work from scratch to create something new. And, sometimes I have to do boring things, like test theories."

They both laughed, Wolf knew she was probably never bored. The flush on Caroline's face as she spoke about what she loved was sexy as hell. Wolf couldn't believe he'd ever thought this woman plain.

It was during a lull in their conversation they both heard the man sitting by the window snort in his sleep. Caroline put her hand over her mouth to keep from laughing too loud and waking him up. She couldn't contain her giggles though and loved sharing a laugh with the big bad SEAL sitting next to her.

Caroline was pleasantly surprised with the conversation with Matthew, who was even more appealing now. Too many times good looking men thought they were God's gift to women and acted that way as well. She'd met some SEALs when she lived in California that were obnoxious because they thought every woman should be throwing themselves at them.

Matthew was interesting and he'd actually listened when she talked. God, she had to get herself together. They were two strangers on a plane. Once they landed in Norfolk they'd go their separate ways and never see each other again. He was just being polite. It was disappointing, but it was just the way it was.

Continuing to talk while waiting patiently for the flight attendant to come by their row with their complementary drinks, Wolf and Caroline shared how they were both sad to leave the nice weather of San Diego—Caroline for good, and Wolf for whatever time he'd be on his new mission.

Finally the flight attendant made it to their row. Caroline was thirsty and was glad to see the drink cart. The attendant still seemed to be a bit sullen and didn't engage people in conversation. Asking the people in the row ahead of them what they wanted to drink and silently serving them, he did the same when he got to their row. The man next to the window had woken up and asked for vodka on the rocks. Caroline ordered a diet soda and Wolf requested an orange juice. Each was given a cup filled to the brim with ice and their drinks, while the flight attendant moved past them to continue serving the rest of the plane.

Caroline poured her drink into the cup and lifted it to take a sip. Suddenly, she stopped. What the hell? She brought the cup to her nose and inhaled deeply. Quickly placing it back on her tray, Caroline saw Matthew was about to drink from his plastic cup. Without thinking how intimate or odd it might seem, Caroline reached over, grabbed the top of Wolf's cup and lowered it to the small tray in front of him.

Chapter Five

WOLF TWISTED IN surprise as Caroline lowered his drink to the tray. What the hell was she doing? He'd thought they were getting along, but damn, he didn't really know her well enough for her to be touching his drink and invading his personal space like that.

He looked over at her, ready to question her, and was surprised to see she was quite pale.

"Don't…," was all she said at first. Wolf could tell Caroline was trying to get her thoughts together.

Wolf's senses went on alert. Whatever was going on had this woman on edge. Feeling bad about thinking she was overstepping her bounds a second ago, Wolf looked at Caroline more closely and saw goose bumps up and down her arms. Shit. Whatever she was thinking was serious.

Matthew gave her the time she needed to gather her thoughts, which Caroline appreciated. Without him asking again what was wrong, Caroline leaned close to him and cautioned in a soft urgent voice, "Something's wrong with the ice. I can smell it. It smells off, like something's in it."

Wolf picked up his drink again and raised it to his face. He could see Caroline wanted to stop him, but she didn't. Pretending to take a sip he smelled it as she had... nothing. He couldn't detect anything but the orange juice that was in the cup. He looked at her and said softly, "I don't smell anything."

Caroline was frustrated. She could tell Matthew wanted to believe her, but when he hadn't noticed anything off about his drink, he was having a hard time. She looked away. Great, now he thought she was nuts. But she wasn't. She was a chemist dammit, and this is what she did for a living. There was some other chemical in with the drink, she knew it. But how would she convince him without sounding crazy?

She turned back to Matthew, only to see him still looking at her.

"What is it?" he demanded softly. "Explain, so I can understand."

Caroline's respect for Matthew rose. He wasn't sure he should believe what she was saying, but he was smart enough to give her time to convince him, and she knew she'd have to explain it in a way he could understand.

Caroline knew she had to get through to him and did her best to convince him she knew what she was talking about. Lowering her voice even further so the people around them wouldn't hear her, she leaned into him and looked him in the eyes as she spoke. "I don't know, but as a chemist I'm trained to pick up on the different chemical smells of compounds. I don't know what it is, but it's not natural."

"Is it in mine too?" he asked her just as softly, passing his cup over to her.

She sniffed it and immediately nodded.

"Shit," Wolf said under his breath. He believed her. He wasn't a person to trust easily, but this woman didn't have any guile in her at all. She'd have no reason to lie to him. Caroline had too much pride as a chemist to pretend something was wrong, he could tell that just from talking to her for the last hour. Besides he couldn't think of what she'd get out of it even if she was lying, and she was obviously freaked the hell out.

His next thought was what the hell was going on with the plane? If Caroline was right, who was trying to drug the passengers on the plane? Who was in on it? Was it all the passengers or just him and Caroline? Was he targeted? Were Mozart and Abe targeted too? He thought about his teammates for the first time after he'd started talking with Caroline. How far back was the flight attendant with the drink cart? Had they drunk anything yet? Shit, he had to warn them.

Leaning in to avoid the possibility of being overheard, Wolf whispered, "Stay seated. I need to warn my men."

Caroline watched as Matthew put his drink on her tray and secured his tray back into the seat back. She didn't ask any questions as he stood up and reached into the overhead bin. He reached for his bag, took his time looking through the small duffle he'd placed up there, then latched the compartment and sat down again.

Wolf felt a bit better after settling back into his seat. He'd signaled to Mozart and Abe that there was danger and not to eat. They'd come up with the signal after being holed up while on a nasty mission and found that the food they were being served was drugged. His men would know something was up, but how to get word to them for sure?

Caroline was watching him closely. Could he use her? No, not use her, but have her help him? He hadn't refastened his seatbelt, so he turned in his seat so he was angled toward Caroline. He took one of her hands into his own, absently rubbing his thumb over the back of her hand as he thought about how he wanted to approach her with his plan. Finally he sighed and looked into her eyes. Caroline was watching him intently. Her big brown eyes were wide and slightly dilated. Her grip on his hand told him she was more scared than she looked.

Wolf's protective side was fighting to come out. He felt and could see the quivers taking over her body. He wanted to stuff her under the seat and tell her not to come out until they were on the ground safe and sound, but he also, unfortunately, knew that wasn't an option. He needed her.

"Caroline, I need your help," he admitted to her softly. He watched as she nodded immediately. Jesus, she didn't even ask what he needed help with, just immediately agreed. He felt something inside shift, but wrestled it down. Now wasn't the time.

"My men are seated in seats 18C and 24D. I need to tell them what's going on, but since we don't know what's really up or who's involved I need to keep it quiet. Will you help me?"

"Of course, Matthew," Caroline told him, her voice only shaking a little. "Although I'm not sure what I can do. I'm just a civilian…"

Wolf squeezed the hand he was still holding, "That's why this'll work. No one will think twice about you walking in the aisles. If I suddenly got up and went back to talk to my teammates, I would definitely be noticed. I'm going to write a short note, if you get up and go to the restroom in the back of the plane, you can pass it to Mozart, who's in 18C."

"Mozart?" was Caroline's comment.

Wolf smiled a bit, chuckling inside that in the middle of a serious scary situation, Caroline still had the presence of mind to question Mozart's name.

He explained quickly, "It's his nickname, we all have one."

Caroline nodded, she wanted to know what his nickname was, but knew this wasn't the time or the place. Maybe someday she'd pluck up the courage to ask him about it…if they got out of this…whatever *this* was. Remembering there were two of his friends on the plane she questioned, "What about your friend in row twenty-four?"

Wolf put his other hand over where their hands were still clutched together. "When you pass him, grab his shoulder instead of the seat and press your second and fourth fingers down hard." He demonstrated on the back of her hand he was holding. "He'll know what it means."

Wolf expected Caroline to ask what the gesture meant, but she didn't. She only nodded her head and demonstrated the hand signal back to him. "Like this?" she asked.

Wolf nodded with approval and couldn't help himself. He lifted her hand that was still clutched tightly in his own and kissed the back of it, holding his lips there for a moment longer than was socially acceptable, before letting go.

"That's all you need to do, then come right back here after you go into the restroom," he told her seriously, looking into her eyes, willing her to understand the danger she was in, that they were all in. "Don't try to be a hero. If something goes wrong, don't worry about it. Just continue on as normally as you can. Don't bring any undue attention to yourself. My guys know something is up and will look out for you. They can see you're sitting next to me so when you get up they'll be on alert. Do you have any questions?"

Caroline shook her head. She was nervous, but she could do this. She wanted to sit and digest the kiss Matthew had planted on the tender skin on the back of her hand, but she didn't have time. She knew if she *did* have the time, she'd probably overanalyze it, and besides she had to concentrate on not chickening out of what Matthew needed her to do.

Matthew quickly scribbled on a piece of napkin. His writing just looked like gibberish to Caroline, so she knew it was in code, but it didn't really matter. She knew he'd probably summed up the situation in a way his friends would be on alert and would be ready to do…whatever. Hopefully it made sense to the man in row eighteen. His other friend wasn't getting an actual paper message, but hopefully whatever pressing her fingers into his shoulder meant, he'd understand. There were so many "hopefullys" in what she was about to do, but they had no other choice. Matthew tucked the napkin into her hand and squeezed it closed gently.

"You can do this, Caroline," Wolf whispered.

It was time. Caroline stood up and flattened herself as much as she could to squeak past Matthew. He didn't want to get up again and bring too much attention to himself. She felt his hand on her waist as she squeezed by. The heat from his hand was intense, but she tried to ignore it. But holy hell, if they were anywhere other than here, in this particular situation, she knew she'd be a complete mess. As much as she wished Matthew was touching her in a sexual way, he was just trying to be reassuring; he wasn't putting the moves on her. She had to force her brain to concentrate though. It just wanted to replay his hands on her body.

18C, 18C, Caroline repeated to herself as she made her way down the aisle toward the back of the plane. She vaguely noticed the other passengers enjoying their free drinks without a care in the world. Caroline had no idea if their drinks were drugged as well, but she had a bad feeling they probably were. She had to make sure she delivered the note to the right person. The last thing she needed was to trip into the wrong person and have someone get the napkin with the weird code. She looked at the seat numbers as she passed them, concentrating hard on making sure she didn't screw up.

She knew right off who Mozart was. She shouldn't have worried about counting the rows. He looked as big and hard as Matthew. Just as she got near him she "tripped," and reached out with her hands to stop her fall, right into Mozart.

"I'm so sorry," she cried out apologetically as she extricated herself from his arms, taking her hands off of his chest where they'd landed. "I'm so clumsy!"

The man simply nodded and helped her right herself. He didn't actually say anything to her, and Caroline found herself blushing, as if she hadn't fallen into him on purpose. She had to get herself together. Sheesh. These sexy men were going to be the death of her.

She straightened, brushed herself off, and continued on her way to the restroom. She took a deep breath. One message delivered, one to go. She'd pressed the note into Mozart's chest when she fell, and she'd felt him grab it when he'd steadied her. She wanted to laugh; it seemed she was pretty good at this cloak and dagger stuff.

Caroline figured she might as well actually use the restroom while she was in the back of the plane. Who knew when she might get another chance with whatever was happening. The practical side of her mind never turned off. She arrived at the restroom in the back just as the flight attendants were finishing up the drink service. Squeezing past the guy who'd served their drinks with an apologetic smile, Caroline closed the restroom door, quickly got down to business, and washed her hands once she was done.

Just as she was going to leave the bathroom, Caroline heard two men talking right outside the door. She paled after hearing their conversation and waited until they'd moved away. Jesus. They were pretty dumb talking about their plan like that where people could overhear them. Caroline supposed they figured soon everyone would be passed out, so it didn't matter. She had to get back to Matthew and tell him what she'd overheard. Crap.

She left the bathroom and didn't look back at the galley; she just walked back toward the front of the plane, grabbing the seatbacks as she went down the plane. When she got to row twenty-four, without missing a beat, she nonchalantly grabbed the shoulder of the man sitting in the aisle seat with her right hand as she walked by, then continued up to her seat. Matthew was waiting and again, assisted her to her seat with a hand on her waist, looking at her questioningly. Caroline nodded once and sunk heavily into her chair. She reached for her seatbelt, but Matthew stopped her.

"Leave it off, just in case," he told her. Caroline nodded again. Crap, she should've thought about that. She wasn't thinking straight. She had to get herself together.

"Matthew," she stated urgently, "before I left the restroom I heard two of the flight attendants talking. They said everything was in place and as soon as the passengers were out, they'd start."

Chapter Six

WOLF DIDN'T SAY anything, just grabbed Caroline's hand, squeezed it and settled it on his leg. Holy crap, what had they landed in the middle of? He absentmindedly rubbed his thumb over the back of her hand while he thought about what the hell was going on.

He felt better knowing Mozart and Abe were alert and ready. Thank God they were on this flight with him. They had very little chance of breaking up whatever was going on here, but at least with all three of them they at least *had* a slim one. He was keyed up and ready to go, to do *something*, but they didn't know who the players were yet.

Obviously two of the flight attendants were in on whatever it was since Caroline had overheard them talking about their plan, but who else? They had to sit and wait and see. He hated that. Wolf thought about 9/11 and wondered if the people on the planes that had been crashed into the World Trade Center had known something was wrong. It was a helpless feeling. The passengers on the plane that had crashed that day in Pennsylvania obviously did what they could to prevent the plane from crashing into the White House, but unfortunately lost their lives in the process.

Wolf didn't want to die, but he knew he could at any time. His job wasn't the safest. Ironically, he was supposed to be on vacation and he was in just as much danger as he was when he was on a mission. It was crazy.

Wolf turned toward Caroline.

"You were amazing," whispered Wolf. "You pulled that off even though you were scared and you didn't bring attention back to yourself or me."

Caroline didn't respond with more than a quick smile. Wolf knew he wouldn't have been able to pull off what she did and not bring attention to himself. Hell, he wouldn't even *know* he was in the middle of a situation if it hadn't been for her. He hated she was going through this, and loathed even more the thought of her not making it through whatever was going on.

Wolf thought more about the situation and was aware the plane had gone pretty quiet. Oh, it hadn't been loud to begin with, but it was obvious what little conversation there had been, had dwindled off. He moved his head a fraction of an inch and saw the three people in the seats across from him had their eyes closed and were sleeping...or worse. He had no idea if they were unconscious, sleeping or even dead.

Just as he was about to tell Caroline they had to lay low and see what was going to happen next, she surprised him by beating him to it.

"Matthew, we have to pretend to have finished our drinks and that it affected us just like everyone else." She'd obviously noticed the other passengers' stillness as well.

Wolf nodded. "I was thinking the same thing. Great minds think alike." He watched as she blushed. She constantly amazed him. The women he'd known in his life didn't blush at a simple backhanded compliment. He thought it was a shame he didn't have the time at the moment to see what other compliments he could give her, just to watch her face light up in the charming blush that was currently covering her cheeks. He tamped down the thought of just how far down that blush went. Wrong time, wrong place, but God he wanted to know.

Caroline took her hand out of his reluctantly, and laid her head back on the head rest. She didn't dare open her eyes to try to see what was going on. They had to pretend to be just as unconscious as the other passengers. She knew Matthew had also tipped his head back and closed his eyes. They just had to wait.

Caroline hated waiting. She was terrible at it. She always got antsy. Her mom always teased her about not being able to sit still for even five minutes when she was little. She was always on the go. Caroline smiled internally at the memory of a story her mom loved to tell guests about when Caroline was about four years old. They'd been at an amusement park and there were long lines for everything; the food, the rides, and of course, the bathroom.

Apparently Caroline had had enough of waiting in the lines, and when they were waiting to use the restroom she'd gone right over to the grass alongside the building and pulled down her pants and peed right there. Caroline's mom was mortified, but everyone else around them had thought it was hysterical.

Caroline thought sadly of her mom. She missed her. So many times in the last year she'd wanted to pick up the phone just to talk. She'd known she would lose her parents far too early in her life, they were older, after all; but it was harder than she thought it'd be.

Pulled from her thoughts by Matthew shifting in his seat, Caroline admitted she was scared. Scared of what was going on and she had no idea how they'd get out of it. It couldn't be good to be trapped in a plane thousands of feet above the ground with people hell-bent on causing trouble. What that trouble was, remained to be seen.

Caroline thought about how glad she was Matthew was sitting next to her. At first she'd been apprehensive; he was a big man after all. But the gentle way he'd held her hand and how he'd immediately taken action to warn his teammates made her feel so much better. She had no idea if he and his buddies would be able to get them out of this, whatever *this* was, but just the fact he was here, made her feel not quite so lonely. She had no idea what she would've done if he hadn't been there. She would've noticed the smell of the ice, but wouldn't have known what to do and would've just had to have sat there, helpless. She shivered a little bit. God. This really sucked.

Thirty long minutes after they'd agreed to act passed out, the terrorists made their move. Almost all of the passengers sat in their seats not moving, either passed out or more. Wolf couldn't waste time thinking about them now. He thanked God for Caroline smelling whatever was in the ice. He shuddered to think about what would've happened if he hadn't been sitting next to her. Actually he knew what would've happened, he and Mozart and Abe would be passed out in their seats, just like all the other people around him now.

Wolf watched as two passengers and the two flight attendants passed by their row of seats and walked toward the front of the plane. He closed his eyes as the two of them then walked back through the plane, examining the passengers, making sure they were all unconscious. Wolf heard them talking quietly as they passed by him.

"Does Smythe have the coordinates?"

"Yeah, as soon as we contain the passengers that are awake, he'll go and take care of the pilots and put us on course."

Wolf tensed. Shit.

The few people the terrorists found awake, they made get up and go to the back of the plane to the galley. Wolf heard some women scream and cry, and grunting from some of the men, but mostly it was a quiet operation. Eerily quiet. In all the battles and missions he'd been in, Wolf had never heard anything like it. Usually people were screaming and crying and there were the loud sounds of gunfire and mortars going off—not this silence and complete compliance from the passengers. It unnerved him, and with his history, that was saying a lot.

He kept his eyes opened only in slits, and watched as one of the terrorists, who'd been posing as a normal passenger, and one of the flight attendants made their way into the cockpit. It was easy since one of the flight attendants simply knocked on the door and requested to talk to the pilot. Since he had no reason to be alarmed, the co-pilot opened it without hesitation. He was immediately beaten bloody while the pilot was killed outright. It wasn't hard, just a quick slice to the jugular. His body was dragged out of the cockpit and thrown into the galley at the front of the plane—still jerking and bleeding out. The co-pilot was alive, but badly hurt. The other flight attendant calmly hefted up one of his legs and callously dragged him to the back of the plane with the other alert passengers.

Wolf's heart rate sped up in preparation for the fight to come. He had to be careful, as one of the terrorists was now at the controls of the plane. He'd been trained by the Navy the basics of flying almost any type of aircraft. He was most comfortable behind the stick of a helicopter, but he'd also spent some time in a big commercial plane like this one. He knew since he was closest to the cockpit, it'd be up to him to get up there and gain control of the airplane.

Mozart and Abe could also fly the plane, but Wolf would rely on them to take care of the other terrorists. He'd have his hands full as it was. He sincerely hoped none of the other passengers were hurt in the process of taking back over the plane, but he couldn't think about that now. His one and only goal was getting back control of the plane.

Wolf knew he had to get going, but for the first time as a SEAL he hesitated. He didn't want Caroline anywhere near what was about to go down, but he had no choice in the matter. He surreptitiously moved his hand and placed it on her thigh and squeezed, feeling her muscles clench under his palm. Caroline's hand came over slowly where it had been resting in her lap and covered his. They sat like that for a moment, both feeling better after the short, but intense contact. Wolf knew it was time to go. He couldn't wait anymore, all their lives depended on it. He turned his hand over so he could grasp Caroline's hand in his and gave it one hard squeeze. Seeing Caroline's small smile, she mouthed, "Good luck." Wolf immediately let go and took a deep breath. It was time.

Without looking around or saying another word, Wolf sprang from his seat and toward the front of the plane. In full battle mode, he blanked all extraneous thoughts out of his head, including the courageous woman he'd left sitting in his row. As he ran toward the front of the plane, Wolf heard a cry and managed a quick look back to see what the situation was.

Mozart and Abe were fighting with two of the terrorists at the back of the plane, but the third was headed right toward him. The look on his face was pure hatred. Shit. Wolf didn't have time to deal with him and make sure the fourth didn't crash the plane. For a second he hoped the guy now piloting the plane didn't know what was going on, but when he felt the plane lurch downward, he knew that thought was futile. Wolf had no choice but to continue toward the pilot. He'd deal with the guy coming up the aisle at him when he had to, which unfortunately might be sooner rather than later.

Wolf watched in amazement as suddenly a leg shot

out from a row of seats and tripped the man coming toward him. Caroline! He turned around and ran full force toward the cockpit. Dammit. He wanted to go back to Caroline, but he couldn't stop now. He was scared for her, which was unheard of for Wolf to lose focus as he had, but there was nothing he could do for her now. He had to get control of the plane or they'd all be dead. Her actions just might give him enough time to subdue the man flying the plane before the other terrorist caught up to him.

Chapter Seven

CAROLINE COULDN'T BELIEVE she'd just tripped a terrorist. A freakin' terrorist! She was scared out of her mind. She'd sat next to Matthew and knew he was about to make his move. She could almost feel the tension in his body, the anticipation, the adrenaline being produced in his bloodstream. She wanted to beg him not to go, to stay with her and just let whatever was going to happen, happen. But he was a SEAL. She knew he wouldn't just sit around and let terrorists take over the plane. He'd be in the thick of it. Hell, he and his team would be the only reason any of them lived through this nightmare, *if* they lived through it.

When he put his hand on her thigh, she knew it was time. She couldn't have stopped herself from reaching out to Matthew at that moment if someone paid her a million dollars. She didn't know if she'd ever see him again, but somehow in the couple of hours they'd spent getting to know each other he'd become important to her. All she could do was smile and mouth to him "good luck"—how cliché. It was stupid. She was just another woman to him. Just one more woman who thought he was gorgeous and who wanted to take him home and spend hours in his bed getting to "know" him. Caroline hadn't admitted it until just now, but yes, she wanted him in the worst way. God, it was so inappropriate and it wasn't going to happen, but that didn't stop her from wanting him.

She didn't know what to do to help, she desperately wanted to do *something*, but she was just a chemist, not a kick-butt SEAL. Caroline watched as Matthew sprung up from his seat. A relaxed sleeping man one second and a raw on-a-mission SEAL the next. He leaped for the front of the plane and Caroline peeked back between the seats to see that Matthew's teammates were busy with two bad guys in the back of the plane. They'd clearly jumped into action right after Matthew had. Obviously Matthew was going up to the cockpit to deal with the terrorist flying the plane.

That left one bad guy unaccounted for. She watched in horror as he came running up the aisle of the plane, headed right toward Matthew. Caroline felt the plane tip down. Her heartbeat tripled. Crap. Crap. Crap. The guy flying was trying to crash the plane. Matthew was about to have to deal with two terrorists, she knew he needed all his concentration to take control of the plane so they didn't die.

Without thinking she slipped over to the aisle seat and when the terrorist was about to run by, she simply stuck out her leg. Damn, that hurt her more than she thought it would. She saw people trip people all the time on TV and in the movies, she had no idea that it'd hurt as much as it did.

The guy went down like a sack of flour. He landed hard on his hands and knees but Caroline knew he wasn't going to stay down for long, so without thinking about the consequences, she leaped out of her seat and latched onto his back. She just had to keep him busy until one of Matthew's teammates could come and help. At least she hoped one of the other guys would come up and help her soon…

Just as Caroline thought she had a good grip on the man, he flipped her over his head into the aisle and scrambled over her until he was on top of her and they were face to face. It'd all happened so quickly she didn't have time to get up or to avoid him.

Shit, Caroline thought looking up at the man. He was pissed, but she was pissed too. The bastard was trying to kill all of them. Caroline flinched away as his fist came toward her face. He managed to hit her in the side of the head, but it would've hurt a lot more if he'd actually made contact with her face. She threw her knee up as hard as she could, and managed to knee him in the thigh. Not where she was aiming, but it slowed him down a bit.

Caroline continued to struggle with the man, each trying to hit and scratch and gain the upper hand. The terrorist out-weighed and out-muscled her, but she didn't let it stop her. She fought like a wildcat. She had adrenaline on her side and a strong wish not to die as well.

Caroline scratched and struck out with her hands and knees and feet. Just as the guy thought he had the upper hand, she'd squirm out of his hold and get in a lucky strike. He was also getting his licks in as well, unfortunately. Caroline wasn't feeling too much pain now, she supposed the adrenaline was preventing any true pain from getting through to her panicked brain, but later she knew she'd hurt…if she had a later.

Any time now someone would come and help her…Caroline had to believe that. Suddenly the weight of the man on top of her lifted and Caroline saw the evil look in his eyes just as a knife cut through his neck. Caroline had to close her eyes as blood spurted out and splattered her chest and arms. It was warm and smelled coppery. Caroline supposed she should've been more freaked out, but she was just so thankful to be alive and to have prevented this man from getting to Matthew. Thank God one of his teammates had finally come to her rescue.

Caroline watched as the man Matthew called Mozart, yanked the man off her, practically threw the now-dead terrorist behind him into the aisle, and leapt over her toward the cockpit. He'd completely ignored her, but Caroline didn't care. She was just glad Matthew would have some help if he needed it. There was no time for introductions or questions in the middle of a terrorist attack. She vaguely heard some of the women in the back of the plane crying hysterically, and knew she had to get up off the floor. If nothing else, the aisle had to be cleared.

Caroline sat up slowly, only then realizing her side hurt. Well, actually, everything hurt, but her side *really* hurt. Caroline looked up and knew now wasn't the time to dwell on it. The women in the back of the plane were hysterical, Matthew's other teammate, from row twenty-four, was trying to calm the passengers in the back. She could see the two terrorists the SEALs had been fighting, lying dead in the back of the plane. Well, she just assumed they were dead. All she could see of the one dead guy was his feet sticking out into the aisle. He'd been partially dragged into one of the rows of seats. The other lay in the middle of the aisle, much as the dead guy she'd been fighting now was.

The entire scene was surreal. If she wasn't in the middle of it, she'd think it was all a bad dream. All around her the other passengers were either passed out or dead from whatever was in the ice. Other than the women in the back crying, it was creepily quiet. She looked toward the front of the plane; she could see Matthew and Mozart in the cockpit. The door laid smashed open on its hinges; Matthew must've broken it in order to get to the cockpit and the terrorist. Another man lay motionless outside the door, obviously the terrorist who'd been flying the plane. His head was turned toward her, his eyes blankly staring.

Caroline turned her attention away from the eerie stare of the dead man, only to have her eyes wander to the dead body next to her in the aisle. His blood was flowing out of the knife wound to his neck and slowly soaking into the cheap carpet underneath him. Caroline could see the puddle growing bigger with each second that passed.

Caroline slowly pushed herself off the floor, ignoring her aches and pains. She tried to ignore the blood on herself from the terrorist that Mozart had killed. Surprisingly she wasn't freaking out. She had no idea why. She *should* be, but she didn't want to be a nuisance to Matthew and his team. It was vain of her, but she wanted them to think well of her.

Before Caroline could talk herself out of it, she leaned down and grabbed the man that had been trying to kill Matthew, and then her, by his ankles and slowly dragged him to the front of the plane. He was heavy, and it was harder than she thought it'd be to drag him.

She watched, in a fog, as the blood oozing from his neck stained the aisle red as she drug him past the airline rows. She brought him into the galley and draped him over the other man that was already there. She had to get him out of aisle so when they did land, medical personnel could get through to the passengers.

After she'd completed that, she wasn't sure what else she should do. She heard Matthew saying her name from the cockpit. Caroline was still seeing and hearing everything as though she was in a long tunnel...she stuck her head into the cockpit.

"Are you all right?" she heard Matthew ask urgently.

Caroline just nodded numbly.

"Is any of that blood yours?"

Caroline shook her head at the question. She didn't really understand what he was asking, but just shook her head anyway.

"Is the co-pilot okay?"

"Uh, I'm sorry Matthew, I don't know." Caroline could barely string two sentences together. She hadn't even thought about checking on the copilot. Duh, she should have.

In a soft voice meant to soothe, Wolf asked, "Can you go back to check and see if he's in good enough shape to come up here and help?"

Caroline didn't look at Mozart, who was currently sitting in the co-pilot's seat and simply nodded. She spun around to go to the back of the plane, not seeing the concerned look on Matthew's face as she turned away and went to find the injured co-pilot. All she could think over and over was *Matthew needs the co-pilot, Matthew needs the co-pilot, Matthew needs the co-pilot*...she kept repeating it to herself so she wouldn't forget.

When she got to the back of the plane, the other SEAL turned towards her. Caroline couldn't remember if Matthew had told her his name, it was enough that she remembered her errand.

"Matthew needs the co-pilot," she said woodenly to the man. Caroline had no idea if she was making any sense, but he must have understood her because he nodded and turned toward the people huddled in the back of the plane. Caroline didn't know what to do, and eventually just headed back to her seat.

She was scared and the adrenaline she'd been operating on for the last thirty minutes was wearing off. Caroline took the unused napkins from their drinks that they'd stuffed into the pockets in front of their seats and tried to wipe some of the blood off her shirt and arms. She was impressed with her clean up job, thinking she'd been surprisingly successful. As she watched, the co-pilot unsteadily made his way back up toward the cockpit. Mozart came out of the small space not long after and headed back toward his teammate in the back of the plane. On his way through, he noticed her and stopped.

"Are you sure you're all right ma'am?" Mozart asked politely.

"Yes, thank you," she replied not elaborating or looking up from her continued attempt at cleaning the blood off of herself. She just didn't have it in her at the moment.

Mozart paused a moment and stared hard at her. Sensing he hadn't left, Caroline finally looked up and stared right back. What did he want her to say? That she wasn't fine? That she was hurting and scared and wanted *off* this stupid plane? Even though it was all true, none of that would be helpful at the moment, so she kept quiet. She was hanging on by the thinnest thread, willing herself not to freak out. Finally Mozart nodded and continued down the aisle.

Caroline sat in the aisle seat in her row with her feet on the seat and her arms wrapped around her legs. Feeling rebellious, she'd refused to put on her seat belt. If she lived through a damn terrorist attack, she could take the risk of sitting unbelted. She knew it was ridiculous to feel like she had to sit in her assigned seat, it wasn't as if anyone would care where she sat, and most of the other seats still had people in them. She would've sat back in her seat in the middle, but couldn't stand to sit next to the guy at the window. He was slumped over. She could see his chest rising and falling, so she was glad for that. It would be horrifying if all the people all around them were all dead. On the other hand, she was glad they hadn't been conscious for everything that had happened. If the reactions from the few people in the back of the plane were anything to go by, it wouldn't have been a good scene. It would've been a lot harder to deal with everything if there had been hundreds of hysterical and panicking people.

The next thirty minutes were some of the longest in Caroline's life. Somehow they felt longer than when they'd been waiting for the terrorists to make their move. Maybe they felt longer because she didn't have Matthew sitting next to her? He made her feel safe and feel like nothing could hurt her. Now she just felt disconnected and shell-shocked.

Feeling the plane start to descend, Caroline knew they weren't in Norfolk yet, not enough time had gone by, so they must be making an emergency landing somewhere. She looked around again, most of the passengers still hadn't moved. Not able to help herself, and having to know one way or another, Caroline lifted her hand, leaned over and checked the man's pulse sitting by the window. He still had one, although it was faint and weak. Hopefully wherever they were landing had a good hospital. These people didn't deserve to die.

The plane finally touched down. It wasn't the smoothest landing, but they were on the ground.

Caroline waited and heard the co-pilot come over the loudspeaker and explain what was happening in a wobbly voice.

"This is the co-pilot. We've made an emergency landing in Omaha, Nebraska. Everyone who can, please move to the back of the plane. There'll be emergency personnel coming aboard as well as Federal Agents. We'll get everyone off as soon as we can and anyone who needs medical help will get it. Thank God, we all made it."

The plane fell silent. Caroline pushed herself to her feet and made her way to the back of the plane. There were eight civilians in the back besides her—five woman and three men. The men looked like businessmen, and the women...the women were gorgeous. Jesus, where were the ugly people? Oh crap, was *she* the ugly person here? The women were all tall and slender. One had attached herself to the SEAL that been sitting in row twenty-four...Caroline still hadn't learned what his name was, and another was hovering close to the man Caroline knew as Mozart. The other women were huddled with the civilian men. It looked as if they'd all bonded over the horrifying experience, while Caroline was once more left sitting on the outside looking in.

The SEALs had moved through the cabin checking the statuses of the other passengers, but there wasn't a lot they could do for them. Caroline eased past the women hanging all over the SEALs without looking at them, and moved to the back corner of the galley.

The jump seats in the back were already occupied, one with a man and a woman on his lap, and the other with another one of the women, who didn't look inclined to move, so Caroline put her back to the wall and slid down until she was sitting. Curling her knees up in front of her and laying her head on her knees, Caroline figured it'd be a while before they'd be leaving and she just wanted to rest.

Caroline didn't see Mozart and the SEAL whose name she never learned, exchange glances. She was just tired and scared. She wanted a shower to get the rest of the dead guy's blood off of her, but knew that wasn't happening anytime soon.

Hearing the medical personnel arrive on board and organizing the removal of the passengers, Caroline overheard Brandy, one of the women standing in the back with the other conscious passengers, exclaim over Mozart and an apparent knife wound he had.

"Don't worry about me," he'd told her. "It's only a flesh wound, I should know, I'm a medic. Besides, the hospital will have enough to worry about with the other passengers. I'll look at it myself, or get one of my buddies to take a look at it. I'll be fine, don't worry about me, but make sure the EMTs get a good look at *you*, sweetheart, to make sure you're all right."

Caroline silently agreed, admiring him. Thinking about her own throbbing side, the SEAL was right. Even though she was hurting, she was alive and didn't want to be a bother. It probably wasn't even a big deal, just a scratch. The other people on the plane needed medical care more than she did—*they* were unconscious and had ingested who knew what. Caroline wished she could've been more help. If she'd been able to figure out what chemical was put into the ice the doctors would be able to help the passengers quicker, but without her lab, she had no idea.

Finally all of the passengers had been taken off to local hospitals. Caroline had fallen into a half-conscious state—awake, but barely aware of all that was going on around her.

After the plane was emptied of the other passengers, the police and FBI herded the little civilian group in the back of the plane outside so the EMTs could look them over. Caroline watched with detached interest the reactions of the other women and men to the dead terrorists scattered around the plane. They were now covered in sheets, but the blood was still clear on the floor as they walked past and over it.

Caroline didn't think anyone was really hurt, but there was no way the police were going to let anyone get off the plane without at least being looked over. There were too many sue-happy people in the world today for them to let that happen.

When it was Caroline's turn, the EMT wasn't happy with her. "Look, I can see you're favoring your side, let me look at it."

Caroline tried to wave him off. "No, really, it's nothing. I just hit it when I fell on the plane—it's fine."

"I should at least look at it," he insisted.

"Well…" Caroline was about to give in when Brandy, one of the civilian women, piped up from next to the young man.

"Sir? I'm feeling a bit dizzy…do you think I can sit down somewhere?"

When Caroline looked at her, she didn't think she looked sick at all. The woman had her hand wrapped around the EMT's bicep and she was leaning into him, crushing her ample boobs against him.

"Uh, yeah, okay, let me finish up here and I'll be right with you. Please sit on that bumper right there so you don't fall and hurt yourself."

Caroline wanted to roll her eyes. When the EMT turned back to her she could see he was already thinking about Brandy. She put him out of his misery.

"Look, just give me some alcohol wipes or something. I'm not hurt that badly and you can go and see what Brandy needs."

It was ridiculous at how quickly the man agreed with her and pulled out some antiseptic wipes. Caroline thought meanly that it was a good thing she wasn't hurt more badly, she'd probably be lying on the ground bleeding to death and the men around her would still probably ignore her.

After each of the conscious passengers were looked at, the police reassured that no one had any life threatening injuries, and they'd all signed paperwork refusing transportation to the hospital, the group was herded onto a little bus.

As the shuttle bus headed toward the airport, away from the tarmac, Caroline was a little depressed. Matthew, Mozart, and the other SEAL had left in a separate bus to who-knew-where. She watched closely as the SEALs walked to their shuttle to see if Matthew would acknowledge her in any way, and of course he didn't. He and his teammates had their heads together as they walked away without looking back at the plane. She shouldn't have been surprised. It happened to her every day.

It was just the eight passengers left, plus herself. Caroline followed the other passengers onto the shuttle. They were driven toward the terminal and hustled in through a side door into a room in the airport. The federal agents wanted to hear their side of the story.

Two hours later Caroline was ready to scream. She wanted to get away from here. She just wanted to be in Norfolk and have all this behind her. They'd been questioned as a group, then separately. The other passengers had no clue what had happened. They'd told the authorities they were sitting in their seats one minute and the next, men with knives had herded them to the back of the plane and while they heard yelling and such, they hadn't seen anything. No one knew what had made the other passengers pass out.

Caroline just nodded along with whatever the others said. No one paid too much attention to her. She was used to it though and, in fact, had counted on it now. She explained the blood on herself away by saying she'd slipped and fallen in the blood of one of the terrorists. She didn't want to say anything because she knew SEAL missions were notoriously secret. And while this wasn't a mission, they were in the wrong place…or was that the right place, at the right time? She didn't want to spill any of their secrets or anything. She wasn't sure what she was supposed to say or not say. The FBI and whomever else would learn what they needed to from the SEALs themselves, not from her. She wasn't even a player in the whole drama, she told herself. She was just Caroline Martin, a regular citizen.

After the authorities had heard everything the awake passengers knew about the attempted hijacking, they were free to go, after being warned not to talk to the press. *Yeah, right!* thought Caroline… A plane hijacking was big business for the media, *huge*. And she knew there was no way Brandy wouldn't use this experience to get herself on television. Caroline had been glad to hear Brandy and the others didn't know what Matthew and his friends did for a living, but of course there was speculation that they were some kind of military secret agents or something.

Caroline wasn't sure where they were free to go *to*. It was dark outside. The airline employees weren't even there anymore. The airport was deserted except for the odd janitor or two. It was a small town and a regional airport. There were no late night flights out. The group was told flights would resume the next morning and they should be able to get on another plane at that time. Caroline sighed. She didn't have her purse; it was still on the plane. She'd have to wait until they released their luggage so she could use her identification to book another seat to Virginia.

Apparently the airline wanted to put all of them up in a local hotel. The airline employees had told the police when they were done interviewing the witnesses to let them know they could get the shuttle to the hotel and stay free-of-charge. Caroline was glad to hear it, since she didn't have any money, but one look outside the airport made her change her mind.

It was complete pandemonium. There were news trucks and people standing around everywhere. It was a madhouse. The reporters were trying to talk to anyone that was around, hoping they'd have some information about the hijacking they could use on their morning news program. Caroline even saw a CNN truck amongst all the other vehicles.

She wanted absolutely nothing to do with the media. It wasn't as if she was afraid to talk to them or anything, she was just exhausted from everything that had happened that day. The fight with the terrorist in the aisle was finally taking its toll on her—she was tired and hurting. All Caroline wanted to do was find a dark corner and shut her eyes. No, what she really wanted was a bath and to talk to her mom, but since she couldn't have either, she'd have to make do with a dark corner where she wouldn't have to talk to anybody.

Caroline watched as Brandy and the other women tried to straighten their already impeccable hair and clothing and got a light of determination in their eyes. They'd seen the media vultures and were thrilled to be able to be in the spotlight. Ignoring the orders not to talk to the press, the small group of witness quickly left the lobby and entered the fray. No one looked back at the quiet, plain woman walking back into the depths of the airport.

Chapter Eight

WOLF, MOZART, AND ABE settled into a booth at the bar at the hotel. They'd spent an hour going over what had happened over the phone with their commander, then another hour going over it again with the FBI agents. Most of their actions were downplayed as their profession required, so the story the FBI received was a watered down version.

But now they were alone and could debrief amongst themselves. While they'd discussed what had happened with the authorities, now they could talk to each other and get the real story, something they hadn't had time to do before now.

"How did you know what was going on Wolf?" Mozart asked in a low voice so no one around would overhear. They all knew if they'd taken a drink most likely everyone on the plane would be dead—them included. It was a sobering thought, but nothing they hadn't been through before.

Wolf shook his head. "I didn't. It was Caroline."

"Who?" Abe asked confused.

"The woman sitting next to me. The brunette."

"The one who gave us the messages," Mozart offered with certainty.

Wolf nodded. "She's a chemist and smelled something off with the ice. She wouldn't let me drink my orange juice."

The men were quiet and digested what Wolf said, realizing they owed their lives to the woman. While they were used to using whatever they had to in order to be successful, none of them could remember a time when a civilian woman's actions had unequivocally saved their lives.

The threesome continued to discuss what had happened. Abe and Mozart had also seen the effect the drinks had on the other passengers and were biding their time until Wolf was ready to move. They'd instinctively known Wolf would take the terrorist in the cockpit out since he was closest to the front, just as the others would take out the remaining men.

"What happened to the third man while you were taking care of the other two?" Wolf asked.

"He was in the aisle fighting with that woman," Mozart answered. "I took care of him and went up to assist you. You know the rest, she was up front and you asked her to get the co-pilot."

"Was she hurt?" Wolf asked Mozart, regretting he

hadn't been able to talk to Caroline after everything had started happening.

"I don't think so. I asked if she was okay when I went to the back, she nodded, but I didn't get to talk to her after that." Mozart replied nonchalantly.

"What do you think she said to the Feds?" Abe asked quietly. They knew they hadn't done anything wrong, but at the same time, they didn't want to be the subject of the media's attention either. They had a job they had to do in a couple of weeks and media attention wouldn't be good.

"I have no idea, but they didn't come in asking us more questions, and there was no media when we checked in," Mozart said thoughtfully.

"About that...did you guys sense anything weird about the Feds that interviewed us?" Wolf asked his teammates.

"Yeah, I was going to bring that up. They seemed more interested in how we knew what was going down than about who the terrorists were or how they managed to get those knives on board." Abe had spoken, but all three men knew something was off.

Mozart added his say as well. "It's obviously important to know how we found out about their hijacking attempt, but it's also very strange they didn't spend as much time trying to figure out how it was all planned."

"I'll talk to the commander when we land in Norfolk. Tell him our concerns and see what he can figure out. It's horrible timing with our upcoming mission though. We don't have time to look into it ourselves. Besides there's no way the Feds will talk to us about it. We'll have to leave it in the commander's hands." Wolf was frustrated. They were missing something, but he didn't know what. If they were back at the base, they'd be able to spend more time trying to figure it out. Wolf had been so looking forward to this vacation, and now he didn't think he'd be able to enjoy it. He'd do what he could from Virginia to look into it though. His gut was screaming at him, there's no way he could drop it.

The men heard a commotion at the bar. They looked over and saw a couple of the women from the plane and two of the businessmen. They were laughing loudly and had obviously imbibed a few too many alcoholic beverages. Obviously this was the hotel the airlines had sent them to after they were allowed to leave the airport. The SEALs had been quietly offered a free room after they'd talked to the authorities, and they'd gladly accepted it. It was obvious the other passengers had also most likely been put up for free as well.

"They are *hot*," Abe said, watching the women, always on the prowl for a one night stand. "Until we had to leave the blonde on the right was into me." He laughed. "Guess she found someone else huh?"

"Where's Caroline?" Wolf asked, more to himself than to his teammates, but they heard him anyway.

"I'm sure she's here somewhere. Man I'm tired and could use a few hours sleep. You guys coming up?" Abe asked, dismissing Wolf's concerns about Caroline as if he didn't even remember meeting her.

As the three men headed up to their rooms Wolf couldn't help but continue to ponder why Caroline wasn't around. She'd been amazing. She was the hero in the whole situation in his eyes. Without her, they'd all be dead. Hell, hundreds of passengers would be dead.

He recalled when he'd looked back and saw her fighting with a terrorist, a *terrorist* dammit. He couldn't believe she'd actually stuck her leg out into the aisle to trip the guy as he made his way toward him. It was a stupid thing to do, and he knew it had to have hurt.

Wolf had been scared for her and felt helpless because he couldn't aid her. He wished he'd been able to talk to her before they'd left, but he didn't have time. As soon as he landed the plane he, Mozart, and Abe had to get their story straight before they met with the Feds. He hadn't even thought about checking up on Caroline before he'd left the plane. Suddenly he felt bad about that. Had she watched him leave? What did she think? Did she even care?

Wolf wondered again where she was. Was she okay? He suddenly felt an urgent need to talk to her. To make sure she was all right. Everything had happened so quickly and he just wanted…he didn't know what he wanted. He hoped he'd see her tomorrow. She said she was going to Norfolk, so she had to be at the airport tomorrow. Their commander told them he was sending a military bird to pick them up in the morning, but maybe he'd see Caroline at the airport before they left. He made a vow to himself to leave early enough in the morning so they'd have time to scope out the civilian side of the airport and see if he could find her and thank her.

CAROLINE WASHED AS much of her face and hands and arms as she could in the restroom at the airport. It was mostly deserted with the occasional passenger here and there, and of course the cleaning crews busily going about their business. She was hungry and wanted to brush her teeth, but had no money, and certainly no toothbrush, but it didn't matter if she had a thousand bucks…the stores were all closed.

Caroline turned her shirt inside out to try to hide some of the dried blood. She didn't really want to put the terrorist's dried blood next to her skin, but she also wanted to blend in. And blending in with others trumped feeling squeamish. Besides, she didn't have any other clothes to wear, so she had to deal with the shirt she had.

The cut on her side was bleeding sluggishly, even after she'd used the antiseptic wipes the EMT had given her, but Caroline didn't think she was in any imminent danger. It hurt, but again, there wasn't anything she could do about it now. She'd go to the doctor when she got to Norfolk. She'd be just fine. Thinking for a moment about heading to the hospital there in Nebraska, Caroline dismissed the thought almost as soon as she had it. All they'd do was probably put a few steri-strips on it and it'd be fine in a few days anyway.

One reason she didn't want to go to the hospital here was that it'd probably be absolutely crawling with reporters trying to get the scoop on the passengers. Second, just as Matthew's friend had said to the woman on the plane, the hospitals were too busy here to need to deal with her little cut. Third, at this point she just wanted to get to Norfolk. Caroline also hated hospitals. If she could at all avoid having to go to one, she would. She'd spent enough of her life cooped up in one for her to voluntarily check herself into another now. As long as she was upright, mobile and her arm wasn't hanging off, she'd self-medicate.

Wadding up some paper towels and holding them to her side as she left the ladies room, Caroline searched for a place to lie down for the night. Thank God the airport police were keeping the reporters out. Maybe, just maybe she'd be able to sleep a couple of hours. She found a dark empty gate and made her way to the edge. Crap. The seats all had arm rests that weren't removable, and she had no desire to sleep sitting up.

Giving up on finding a comfortable seat, Caroline eased herself down to the floor, turned onto her side and made sure the wadded up paper towels were pressed to her side against the floor. Hopefully the pressure of her body against her side and the paper towels would have the sluggish bleeding stopped by morning.

Caroline closed her eyes and tried to block out the images that bombarded her. She saw the terrorist's eyes right before his throat was slit; she saw the stranger sitting next to her slumped over against the window; she saw herself tripping a freaking terrorist and watching as he flew through the air. She saw the sightless eyes of both the pilot and the terrorist that had been flying the plane. Also whipping through her mind as if she was watching a movie and not simply recalling events that had actually happened to her were scenes of Matthew holding her hand and running his thumb over her knuckles. She saw the tender look in his eyes as he asked if she was okay while he was sitting in the cockpit. Finally she saw him walking away from the plane without a second glance.

Chapter Nine

THE MILITARY PLANE wasn't leaving until early afternoon so the SEAL team had a leisurely breakfast—as leisurely as it could be with the shouts and lights from the media outside the small hotel—and watched as two women from the plane and the men headed out the door to go back to the airport to see if they could catch another flight.

Abe heard them talking before they left about how irritated they were that the airline and Feds hadn't given them their bags back yet. The men had their wallets in their pants pockets, but the women's purses were still on the plane. That got Abe thinking about the woman who'd saved all their lives. He'd been thinking more about her last night. Yesterday had been crazy, but he'd had time to think now, and he was ashamed of himself and his fellow teammates.

"About the woman…" he blurted out when they'd all sat down at breakfast.

Wolf and Mozart looked at him with surprise.

"What about her?" Wolf snapped, somehow knowing Abe was talking about Caroline and Wolf was feeling possessive for no good reason he could think of. But he knew there was no way he was letting Abe make a move on Caroline if that was what he was getting at. He was way too slick with the ladies and hadn't ever had a lasting relationship. He didn't want to think of Caroline being just another conquest for Abe.

"SEALs don't leave SEALs behind. Ever." It was their motto. The thing that every SEAL learned throughout Hell Week and BUD/S training. "Why do I feel like we've left a team member behind?" Abe asked quietly. Neither of the other men said anything.

"We all heard the women this morning say they didn't have their purses with them. They weren't able to get their stuff from the plane. We didn't see Ice last night and she's not been down for breakfast this morning. Where did she stay?"

"Who?" asked Mozart.

Abe smiled for the first time that morning. "Ice. That's her nickname."

They all nodded, understanding at once how she'd earned the moniker. Without Caroline smelling the ice and knowing something was wrong, they'd all be dead.

Wolf still hadn't said anything, but stood up and gathered his stuff quietly. Mozart and Abe didn't even have to ask what he was doing. They'd been together long enough to know when Wolf decided on a course of action he was all about getting it done. After throwing some bills on the table to pay for the food they'd barely touched, they followed his lead. They were going to find their teammate.

CAROLINE STOOD LEANING against the wall of the airport and watched the chaos around her. She'd slept like crap the night before. Even though the airport was basically deserted, the stupid recording about not parking in the white zone and the possibility of being towed was replayed all night over and over. She had no idea why they bothered to keep it going when there weren't any passengers around to hear it. The recording, along with her nightmares and the pain in her side, kept her from getting a good night's sleep.

When Caroline had woken up that morning she'd felt light headed and weak and wasn't thinking straight. When she'd gone to the restroom and checked out her side, she was dismayed to see that as soon as she took the paper towels away from her side, she started bleeding again. It was red and obviously infected as well. Nice. *The least the terrorist could've done was made sure his knife was clean*, Caroline thought grimly, wincing as she poked the reddening wound on her side.

At least she had some good news that morning—

she'd finally gotten her purse back. Since she was already at the airport she was first in line to reclaim her belongings. All of the passenger's bags were still sitting in the belly of the plane. The airline couldn't release them yet; they were still investigating how the terrorists had smuggled their weapons on board, so everyone's luggage was being searched. She'd been reassured that the bags would eventually be flown to Norfolk once the investigation was over and the airline employee handed her a business card with a small apologetic smile.

Caroline bought a bottle of water and a bagel as soon as the little coffee shop in the airport opened, but when she'd started to eat, she felt nauseous. She hoped she'd be hungry later, so instead of throwing the food away, she tucked it into her purse.

Many of the relatives of the passengers on the plane had been arriving in the little airport all morning. A lot of the passengers had been released from the hospital already. Caroline watched for a while as they ran the gauntlet to try to get into the airport. If possible, it looked like there were even more media trucks and people standing outside. Of course this was a huge media event. An attempted airplane hijacking after the September 11 attack was a huge deal and it was getting coverage from what looked like every country in the world.

All of the passengers who'd decided to brave flying

again, and their relatives, were standing in line to talk to someone from the airline. Everyone wanted to get to Virginia, or at least get to *somewhere*, but of course the airline was putting them all on standby. It seemed to Caroline that the least the airline could do was get another plane here to take care of them all. But she didn't really know anything about how the industry worked, and most likely, it was easier said than done.

Caroline stood against the wall eyeing the line at customer service, waiting for it to go down. She should've gotten in line first thing this morning, that was one of the reasons she'd stayed the night in the airport instead of the hotel, but she'd been hungry and feeling sick, so she'd put it off. Now the line was too long for her to be able to stand in it–not with how much her side hurt. If she'd been thinking clearly she would've realized the line wasn't going to get shorter anytime soon because people were arriving at the airport steadily. So as soon as one person would get seen, another would arrive and get in the back of the line.

Caroline had to get a seat on another plane east, but wasn't sure when the next one would be leaving. Hell, it wasn't as if she'd be able to get on it anyway. Flying standby sucked. She closed her eyes. She'd just rest here against the wall and wait for the line to go down. Surely it couldn't take too long.

Mozart, Abe, and Wolf stalked into the airport not

knowing if they'd find Ice there or not, but they had to try. The reporters were crazy aggressive outside the small building, but the friends waded through the people, refusing to stop and talk to anyone. When they entered, they stopped and looked around the baggage claim area. It was a zoo. Obviously the relatives of the passengers had started to arrive.

"Let's split up and see if she's down here," Mozart said. "Meet back here in ten."

They all set out. Ten minutes later they were all back; there was no sign of Caroline. The airport wasn't that large and the baggage claim area only had three carousels.

The three men headed upstairs to the ticketing area. At the top of the stairs they looked around. There was a customer service desk that had a line that was at least an hour long and two ticket counters, which also had long lines. There were also a few small shops and the entrance to the gates where security screening was set up. The area wasn't large and they could see almost everyone in it. There was a chance Caroline had already gotten past security and was waiting at a gate for a plane, but they had no way of knowing or getting past security to look for her.

Looking around and not seeing any sign of Ice, Mozart said dejectedly, "I really thought she'd still be here."

"We should probably go and catch our ride," Abe

added quietly as disappointed as Mozart was at not finding the woman who'd saved their lives.

Wolf gave them an incredulous look. "Are you guys blind? She's right there," and he turned his back and headed for Caroline. She was standing by herself near a wall with her eyes closed. She was obviously wearing the same clothes as the day before. Guilt hit Wolf hard. Damn.

Even though she looked exhausted and miserable, Caroline looked great to him. Wolf was so damn relieved she was still here he felt his toes tingling. He couldn't wait to talk to her again. He was so gone.

Abe and Mozart were close on Wolf's heels as he headed toward her.

"Damn, I didn't even see her," Abe apologized to Wolf quietly.

"Me neither, Abe," Mozart commiserated. "She doesn't draw any attention to herself does she?"

Wolf reached Caroline first. She hadn't heard him walk up and he didn't want to scare her.

"Caroline?" He whispered.

Caroline was in her own world. Imagining she was sleeping in a big bed when she heard her name. Her eyes flew open. Crap. How had someone snuck up on her? She was obviously more tired than she'd thought.

Her brain realized it was Matthew before her body did, but she couldn't stop herself from lurching to the side and away from the perceived threat. Wolf was ready for her reaction and grabbed her arm to keep her from falling. Caroline could feel his hand brush against her wounded side as he held her arm gently. It took everything in her to not flinch with pain. For some reason she didn't want this incredible man to know she'd been hurt. Caroline and Wolf just looked at each other for a moment then Mozart and Abe were there.

"Here you are! We've been looking for you, Ice," Abe exclaimed.

"For me?" Was all Caroline could get out she was so surprised. "Why?"

"SEALs don't leave SEALs behind. Ever." He said with complete seriousness.

"And? I'm not a SEAL," Caroline said befuddled.

"Maybe not in truth, but you saved our lives, that makes you one of us in our eyes," Mozart answered, completely serious.

Caroline looked back and forth between the three men, confused. She cleared her throat and finally commented, "I assume you guys are all okay?"

Wolf chuckled. "Of course we are. Are *you*?"

"Uh, yeah, I'm okay too," she answered and just looked at them waiting for…something. She still had no idea what they were doing there. She didn't really understand the whole "you're a SEAL" thing. Duh, of course she wasn't. Had they lost their minds?

"What are you doing over here? Do you already have another ticket to get to Norfolk?" Mozart asked breaking the silence between them.

Caroline shook her head to clear it. He'd asked her something. Oh yeah…

"I'm waiting for the line to go down so I can see if I can get on another plane," she explained. "I have to fly standby, but I thought I'd wait a bit for the crowd to thin out."

"Doesn't look like it's going to thin out anytime soon, Ice," Mozart said. "Why don't you come and sit with us for a while?"

Caroline knew she couldn't sit with them. She wasn't used to attention from a man, nonetheless three men who looked like they should be on the cover of *GQ* or *Soldiers of Fortune*. They were gorgeous and were attracting attention by just standing there in the airport. Caroline could see women do double takes as they walked by. She had no idea how they were able to blend in when they were on a mission. There was no way these men could go anywhere unnoticed.

She also knew she didn't feel good, and didn't want them to know. Caroline was embarrassed that a little scratch on her side was making her feel so terrible. She was obviously a wuss. They were strong men, they thought she was one of them, she couldn't show any weakness. Then something Mozart said finally sunk in.

"Ice?"

All three men chuckled again. Geez, having all three of them smiling at her like that made her feel like she was only woman in the room, and that scared her to death.

"Yeah, Abe named you that for your super sniffing skills smelling that ice and knowing what was up," Mozart explained.

Caroline smiled a bit at that. Funny. Then something else occurred to her. This was the first time she'd heard the third SEAL's name. "Abe?"

Abe came forward and took the hand on the arm Wolf wasn't holding, and brought it up to his lips. "I'm Abe. It's good to meet you sweetheart. Thanks for saving our lives."

Caroline nervously pulled her hand back and ignored his over the top flattery. Somehow she knew he probably treated all women the same way. She wasn't special. She also knew if she wasn't able to deal with it when she was one hundred percent, she definitely couldn't deal with it today.

She looked at the three gorgeous men standing around her looking at her with concern. The concern felt good, but she knew it wouldn't last, it never did.

"I can't call you guys by your nicknames. Sorry. It's just too weird. What are your real names?"

Not letting them answer, Wolf told her, "Abe is

Christopher and Mozart is Sam."

"Okay, that's easier for me to remember. I'll call you guys that."

They all smiled at her as if they thought she was cute. Mentally rolling her eyes, Caroline couldn't go around calling these masculine men by the silly nicknames they'd given each other for probably asinine reasons.

Seeing their smiles reminded her that she needed to make them leave. They'd leave soon enough, she might as well hurry them along so she could go and find a seat and feel miserable in solitude.

She looked at each of the men and said in a tone that projected dismissal, "Well, thanks for coming to check on me, but I'm okay and I have to go get in line now. I'm glad you're all okay too. Good luck on your upcoming mission and stay safe. All right?"

She peeled herself away from Matthew and turned toward the line. She waved lamely at the three men, turned her back on them and went to get in line. She couldn't let them stay. She didn't belong with them, she was just plain Caroline. Not Ice, not a part of their team. She was nowhere near their league. She had to leave now before her heart decided it wanted more. Before she let Matthew break her heart.

Mozart, Abe, and Wolf watched as Caroline walked away from them without a second glance and got in line.

"Well, that didn't go well did it?" Mozart asked no one in particular.

Wolf grunted and headed toward the stairs. Fine. If she didn't want them around, they'd go. He didn't understand his feelings of hurt, but he'd never chased after a woman, and wasn't going to start now, no matter how much he wanted to. A little part inside told him he was being an ass, but he ignored it. He'd thought they had a connection, but if Caroline was able to walk away from him that easily, he was obviously wrong.

Caroline held her breath. She didn't really want them to go, especially didn't want Matthew to go, but she didn't think she had a choice. They weren't really interested in her; they were just following up on the incident. She was glad to see that none of them seemed to be hurt though. That was good. Caroline hoped they'd be safe in their upcoming missions. The more she thought about those missions, the more she panicked a little inside. She had no right to worry about them—no right to be concerned. She was a passing oddity for them. Once they got to Norfolk they'd laugh about the entire thing and come to their senses. *Matthew* would come to his senses. He'd realize she was a nobody, a geek, and move on with his life.

Once she knew they were gone, she'd go back and sit down. She couldn't stand in this line much longer.

She already felt dizzy and was still nauseous. She swayed on her feet trying to calculate how much time they needed to disappear and how much time she had left before she fell on the floor in a dead faint.

Abe and Mozart followed Wolf down the stairs. They didn't say anything to him, but they knew he was fighting some sort of demon they didn't understand, so they didn't push him. Of course they figured it was about Ice, but since neither of them had seen him act like that before, they weren't sure what was going on. Wolf was a ladies man, like most of them. He didn't have to work hard to attract women, but lately he seemed out of sorts. He hadn't been out with them for a while and he just didn't seem interested in women…until now. Until Ice.

Mozart took a hard look at Wolf. His hands were clenched at his sides and he strode purposefully down the stairs. They were headed out of the building to another part of the airport where their military bird waited for them. Suddenly Mozart noticed something else, something Wolf and Abe seemed to have somehow missed. He knew they'd be pissed they'd overlooked it. After all they'd been trained to be observant. Mozart couldn't wait to rub it in.

"I'll meet you at the plane," he promised Abe and turned and ran back up the stairs taking them two at a time without any other explanation. Abe had no idea where his buddy was going, but shrugged and followed Wolf out the door. He'd be back soon no doubt.

Wolf sat in the seat on the military airplane brooding. He wasn't sure why Caroline had gotten to him so much, but she had. She was smart and brave and...dammit. He didn't want to leave her. But what choice did they have? Did *he* have? They had a plane to catch. Did he have to leave? What if he stayed and flew commercial with her? He still had some leave time. Shit. His commander had said they had to get to Norfolk and debrief in person. They had to meet with someone there and go over what happened. Wolf knew the entire episode was a security breach and someone had to answer for it.

But Wolf still had a thousand questions for Caroline. What did she tell the authorities, where did she spend the night last night, what had really happened with the terrorist Mozart had killed when he was on top of her? And maybe most importantly, did she want to see him again? Wolf was still brooding about the entire situation when he looked up and saw Mozart escorting the woman he couldn't get out of his mind onto their plane.

What the hell? Mozart knew civilians weren't allowed on official military flights. Wolf stood up to chew him out when Mozart signaled him to "wait." Wolf ran his hand through his hair in frustration. What had he missed? Why did Mozart go back and get Caroline? He wasn't someone to buck authority, ever. But he was now. What was going on? Wolf sat back down and bided his time. He trusted his team, but he wanted to know what was going on now.

He wasn't sure he could handle spending more time with Caroline only to have her rebuff him again. It hurt enough the first time. Yes, it hurt, Wolf admitted to himself. Every instinct he had was screaming at him to get up and go to Caroline, but if Mozart wanted him to wait, it was for a damn good reason. He'd give him a bit of time, but as soon as they were in the air he was going to find out what the hell was going on.

Caroline tried for the tenth time to get Sam to let go of her arm. He wasn't budging. He'd come back up the stairs, straight to where she was standing in line, took her arm and led her away. Away from the airport and to here, this plane. To where Matthew was.

She tried to tell him to let her go, tried reasoning with him, tried making him mad, tried everything she could think of, but he just held on and kept walking. He didn't say anything to her other than, "Come on, Ice, you're traveling with us back to Norfolk." That was it. Nothing else. She didn't even know where they were going once they got to Virginia, but she supposed anyplace beat sitting in the airport going nowhere.

Caroline sat in the seat Sam led her to gingerly. He

helped her get buckled in, then walked further back into the plane to find his own seat. Thank God he hadn't put her next to Matthew. She didn't want him to know she was hurt. It hurt to lean back, so she sat upright in the seat. Surprisingly enough, none of the SEALs came and sat next to her. She'd seen both Matthew and Christopher on the plane, but neither one approached her.

She was glad, but also sad too. Mostly she was confused. As the plane taxied down the runway she tried to relax and not think about hijackers. Nothing was going to happen on this flight. It was a military plane, flown by military personnel with three SEALs on board. There were no flight attendants, only the four passengers and the pilots. She tried to relax, but couldn't. She couldn't get the thoughts of the terrorists out of her mind.

As soon as the plane was airborne and at a relatively safe altitude, Mozart stood up and went to Ice. On his way he signaled to both Wolf and Abe, "injured."

Wolf watched as Mozart got up. He wasn't going to go to Caroline. She didn't want to come with them. With him. He'd be damned if he....just as he was working up a good temper toward her, he saw Mozart's signal. Fuck. Injured? How the hell did he miss it? He got to Caroline about the same time as Mozart. He didn't remember getting up and moving forward, but there he was. *Caroline was injured? What the fuck?*

Mozart let Wolf squeeze by, and as he did told him quietly, "I saw the blood on your shirt from where you grabbed her in the airport." Sure enough, Wolf looked down and saw the tiny smear of blood. He'd missed it. Jesus. Thank God Mozart hadn't. He'd never live it down, but at the moment he couldn't give a damn.

Wolf kneeled down next to Caroline's seat. Her seat belt was buckled, but she was sitting up straight, unnaturally straight. Now that he knew she was hurt, he could see how uncomfortable her position was.

"Caroline, where are you hurt? Let me see."

Caroline shook her head, but didn't look at Matthew. "I'm fine, really…"

Wolf gave a chin lift to Abe and Mozart and signaled for them to get the makeshift cot in the back ready. Like most military planes, this one was equipped with a space in the back for injured soldiers.

"Come on Caroline, up you go. We're going to the back. Let me take a look and make sure you're all right." He reached out and quickly unbuckled her seatbelt, brushing her hands aside when she tried to prevent him from taking care of her.

"Seriously Matthew, I'm okay. I just want to sit here. I'm tired." Caroline whined, trying to resist, but she was too tired and hurting too much to put up more than a token resistance.

"Caroline, please. Let me help you."

It was the please that finally got to her. She sighed and nodded, defeated. He was going to have his way no matter what she said. Besides, they were already airborne; it wasn't as if she could ignore them or walk away.

Wolf helped her to the back and sat her down on a cot. He sat next to her and put his hand over hers on her knee.

"Mozart here is going to take a look." When she struggled a bit and looked like she'd stand up, Mozart leaned down toward her.

"Look at me, Ice," Mozart demanded. At the tone of his voice, Caroline looked up at him, panic in her eyes.

"I'm just going to look. I'm sure you're fine, but at least let me see…okay? I won't hurt you. I *am* trained you know," Mozart said with humor in his voice.

"It's not that…" At their expectant looks she sighed and quipped sarcastically, "Okay, but if you suddenly have the urge to jump me, don't blame me!" She knew what kinds of women these men were used to, tall skinny women without an extra pound on them. She wasn't that, no way, no how. Usually she didn't care, but baring herself to them, especially to Matthew, wasn't something she wanted to do in this lifetime. She couldn't seem to lose the last fifteen pounds that clung stubbornly to her stomach and thighs. She didn't tan, and …she couldn't think of anything else because

Mozart was lifting up her shirt and exposing her stomach and side. She tried to suck in her breath and her stomach at the same time.

"Relax," Wolf murmured next to her head. He tilted her head up so she had to look him in the eyes. "Talk to me Caroline," he commanded.

"Wh-what do you want to know?" She stuttered trying to ignore what Mozart was doing.

"Tell me what happened after I got up to go into the cockpit," Wolf insisted.

Caroline was quiet for a moment, then tried to downplay what had really happened.

"When you got up, the other guy was coming for you so I tripped him. It stopped him for a moment, but you were still busy and he was getting up. I grabbed him to stall him and then Sam came up and killed him." She finished in a rush and looked away from Wolf's eyes.

"Now tell me what *really* happened," he growled. "You're a terrible liar." He paused and when she didn't continue he added, "Please tell me. Caroline, I've been on hundreds of missions for my country, but I don't have the words to express how thankful I am that you were sitting next to me on that plane. Not Mozart, not Abe...*you*. You did what you had to do and you saved my life and the life of everyone on that plane not once, but twice. Now tell me."

Caroline ducked her head. Crap. She hadn't done

anything she was ashamed of, but for some reason she really didn't want to tell Matthew what had truly happened. She couldn't help but feel as if she should have done more. She inhaled a quick breath when Sam did something to her side that really hurt. Damn. She quickly stumbled over her explanation to get it out of the way and to try to take her mind off of Sam's probing.

"The terrorist was on the ground but getting up and you were still trying to get into the cockpit. I knew I had to do something or we'd all die. So I jumped on his back. I tried to keep him down, but he was too strong for me. He flipped me over and we had a kicking and hitting match. I didn't know he had a knife, which was dumb I suppose, but he must have gotten me while we were fighting."

"Why didn't you say anything afterward? Either before we landed or when the paramedics were there? Didn't you see an EMT?" Abe asked suddenly from somewhere off to her uninjured side. Caroline shifted her gaze over to him.

"For the same reason you didn't, Christopher," she explained slowly. "I heard what you told that woman on the plane. She asked why you weren't going to get help. You said the hospitals were busy enough with the other passengers. They wouldn't have had time for you and it wasn't fair to the other passengers. I agreed, and besides it was just a scratch. I got some antiseptic wipes from the EMT and tried to clean it last night. It wasn't until this morning that it started looking red."

There was silence. The three SEALs were actually stunned into silence. Jesus, this woman was braver and less self-serving than a lot of the people they worked with on a daily basis.

Finally Mozart broke the silence and told Caroline, "It looks like the knife missed penetrating very deeply, Ice, but you have a good slice across your side. It's more than a scratch. It's infected. I think you need stitches as well as antibiotics."

Caroline took a deep breath and didn't say anything. She looked up at Matthew and saw him clenching his teeth and working his jaw. She looked away. Why was he mad at her?

"I don't want to go to the hospital. I-I don't like hospitals." Caroline begged, a little desperately. She kept her eyes on the man hovering above her, not able to look at the disappointment she knew she'd see on Matthew's face.

Wolf turned her head back toward him again so she was looking him in the eyes. "Mozart can sew you up, if you'll trust him."

Caroline didn't hesitate, "I trust him. I trust all of you. I just...." She paused. Took a deep breath and continued on. "I just don't want you guys to think I'm a wuss."

She hadn't hesitated to say that she trusted them—that went a long way toward making Wolf feel better. But a wuss? Seriously?

"Ice," Abe said firmly before Wolf could get a word out, "You're not a wuss. In fact I would go so far to say you've held up better than some of the SEALs in training back in San Diego. Let us take care of this for you. You'll be up and around in no time."

Wolf looked at his teammate. Interesting. Abe wasn't known for being the most patient man, especially with women. He knew Abe respected woman and tried to be polite with them, but most of the time he tended to be short and abrupt with women, wanting to be with them sexually, nothing else. But there was something about Caroline that brought out the protective instincts with all of them.

"We'll be right here with you, Ice," Abe promised firmly. Caroline nodded and shut her eyes. Wolf had to distract her. He could see that every muscle in her body was scrunched up tight in preparation for whatever it was she thought Mozart was going to do to her.

"Where did you go last night, Caroline?" Wolf asked.

Caroline answered without opening her eyes. Her eyebrows were still scrunched together as she was waiting for Sam to do something. "Nowhere. I spent the night in the airport."

Wolf's eyes met Abe's eyes guiltily. Abe had been right.

"Why? Why didn't you go to the hotel? Didn't they offer you a comped room?" Wolf asked knowing what the answer was already, but asking anyway.

"Yeah, but I thought I'd just stay at the airport since I'd hoped to leave first thing this morning. Besides, I didn't have any money for anything like food when I got there. They gave us the room for free, but I didn't know if the food came with it or not." Caroline grunted as Sam inserted the needle that would put the anesthetic into her side.

"Hell, why didn't you just ask, Caroline? If you did need money, I'm sure one of the men would have given it to you." Wolf chastised her gently.

Caroline opened her eyes at his tone. She looked him straight in his eyes. She wanted him to *hear* what she was saying. Without looking away from Matthew she asked Christopher a simple question.

"Christopher, when did you first notice me?"

Abe answered without hesitation and laughed a bit. "When you fell on top of Mozart as you walked down the aisle on the plane."

"Sam, when did *you* first notice me?" Mozart was waiting for the anesthetic to take effect and told her honestly. "Same as Abe, I saw you walking down the aisle and of course when you about fell in my lap."

Caroline hadn't looked away from Matthew while the others were answering her question. She directed the same question to him.

Wolf thought back and suddenly he knew where she was going with her question and opened his mouth to lie when she interrupted him, as if she could tell what he was thinking. "And don't lie, Matthew."

Shit. Wolf sighed. "I noticed you when you offered to switch seats with me."

Caroline nodded as if they'd given her the answers she expected.

"Christopher, you and I met at the lunch counter in the airport in San Diego. I was standing right in front of you. You dropped your fork and I picked it up for you. You thanked me and continued to your seat." Abe flushed, remembering the incident now that she'd brought it up, but Caroline wasn't done.

"Sam, you were sitting at the end of a row of chairs with your feet out, I tried to step over your legs without disturbing you, but you noticed anyway, apologized, and moved out of the way. I said it wasn't a big deal, you nodded and I went and sat down in the same row of chairs as you." Caroline still hadn't looked at the other men, but heard Mozart's low, "damn."

Caroline took a deep breath. "Matthew, you and I met on our way into the airport. I was having problems getting my suitcase in the door because one of the wheels was broken and…"

Wolf interrupted her, "…And I helped you carry your suitcase through the door and up to the check-in kiosks." Caroline nodded a bit sadly. "You said you hoped I had a good flight and walked off down toward the security check-point." Except for the roar of the engines there was silence.

"You asked why I didn't ask for help, Matthew," Caroline continued after a beat, "it's because I'm not the kind of woman people notice. The three of you all talked to me, but still didn't remember me. I'm not the kind of woman people recollect or go out of their way to help." All three men went to interrupt her, but Caroline weakly held up her hand to stop them and continued.

"It's okay. I know what I am and what I'm not. What I'm not is like one of those women on the plane. You know Christopher, the blonde that was cozied up to you? The ones that got the men to fawn all over them? Even if I'd asked for help I'd most likely have been turned down. Politely I'm sure, but turned down. In a room full of people, no one notices me. That's just the way it is, and it's *fine*." Caroline emphasized. "So don't any of you feel sorry for me. I didn't ask for help because I knew I'd be fine in the airport for one night. Hell, people spend the night in airports all the time. I just didn't have the energy to care last night. And I don't have the energy right now to be embarrassed about telling you all of this. So don't go reminding me later, okay?" She tried to make the men feel better. She knew they felt guilty, but she didn't want them to. That wasn't why she told them what she had. "I just want you guys to know that I understand why you feel like you have to help me, but I'm fine. I'll be okay." She shut her eyes, not able to look at the guilt she could see in Matthew's eyes anymore.

"I don't think you understand anything about us, Caroline," Wolf countered. He didn't elaborate.

Caroline didn't open her eyes or say anything else. Wolf knew she'd heard him; she just wasn't acknowledging what he'd said.

Mozart poked at her side for a moment and when Caroline didn't flinch, declared to everyone that her side was numb enough to put in the stitches. Wolf stood up and carefully helped Caroline lie down on the cot then kneeled on the floor next to her. She lay on her side. She had one hand under her head and the other was curled up against her chest, as if anticipating the stitches going in.

Mozart actually looked to Wolf for approval before he leaned down and started stitching her side. It wouldn't take too many, but he wanted to be as careful as he could be. Since it was Ice, he wanted to spare her as much pain and make the scar as small as possible.

Abe had left their side for a moment while Mozart stitched her up but he was back with another needle as soon as Mozart was done with his handiwork. Abe also looked to Wolf for his okay before proceeding. Wolf nodded at him. With Wolf's approval, Abe leaned down and stretched out Caroline's arm that had been clenched tightly against her chest. He found a vein on the inside of her elbow and administered the drug before she could do more than put up a token protest.

Caroline turned to look at Matthew in surprise.

Wolf's chest expanded at the fact she'd looked at him for reassurance, not at Abe or Mozart. At her questioning look, Wolf simply said, "To help you sleep."

Caroline nodded but laughed. "I don't think I need any help sleeping, Matthew. I didn't sleep very well last night."

Wolf leaned close to Caroline's head. Damn, she hadn't complained once. She'd been in pain, was in a plane getting stitched up, and she'd let a man she didn't really know inject an un-known drug into her system. Wolf would've beaten her ass if he hadn't been so proud of her for being so strong.

Wolf figured he'd get to ask one more question before she was out. They hadn't had a chance to talk to her about what went on in the interrogation by the Feds. He hated to do it now, but they had to know what everyone said in the civilian's debriefing before they met with the commander in Norfolk.

"What did you say to the FBI about what happened, Caroline?" He wanted to put off the uncomfortable question and possibly bring back bad memories for her, but he knew, as the team leader, this was something they needed to know before any of the personal things could be said.

"Nothing, Matthew," she said sleepily.

"Nothing?" Wolf pressed skeptically.

"Nothing." Caroline confirmed. "They were more interested in the stories from the other passengers. They were willing to talk and say what they knew, which wasn't a lot. They thought you guys were most likely some sort of military, but since they were in the back when most of what happened, happened, they didn't have much to say. While they questioned me, no one really seemed interested. I already told you about me and people not noticing me."

While he was happy she hadn't said anything, it'd make it easier for them to stay under the radar, and he was still baffled by this woman. All three men looked at each other over Caroline's drowsy form. If she'd kept quiet as she'd claimed that should help with whatever was going on with the Feds. They'd been very interested in how and why the terrorist's plan failed; to the point of suspicion. None of the SEALs wanted Caroline put in the middle of whatever was going on.

Mozart asked the question they were all thinking. "Why didn't you tell them what you did, Ice?" he asked quietly from her side.

Caroline tried to open her eyes, but they were just too heavy. *Jesus what was in that shot?* "I didn't *do* anything, *you* guys did all the hard work…and I didn't want to get you guys in trouble." She murmured. "I know what you SEALs do is usually kept hush-hush and I didn't want to say anything that you guys didn't already explain, so I told them nothing. Figured it'd be better." Her voice slurred more and more. "Believe me, I wanted everyone to see how sexy you guys are, and know you're heroes and what you did, but I know that's not how you operate…" Her voice trailed off. She was out.

The three SEALs said nothing as they got Caroline cleaned up and comfortable on the cot. They had to strap her in so when they landed she wouldn't roll off. Mozart had given her enough of the sedative to keep her asleep for a while. Wolf stayed by Caroline's side holding her hand, while Abe and Mozart went and sat in empty seats.

They all had a lot to think about. This slip of a woman had touched each of them in different ways. None of them would be the same. All of them knew they'd protect her with their lives if need be. They didn't know what would happen next, but somehow they knew it wasn't over. Their instincts were screaming at them that something was wrong, but they didn't know how or why. None of them wanted to see Caroline disappear from their lives. She'd become important to them by just being herself. She was unassuming and they were so damn proud of her they couldn't stand it.

Chapter Ten

CAROLINE WOKE UP slowly, feeling like her head was filled with cotton. She rolled over and gasped in pain. Ouch, she'd forgotten about her side. She lifted up her shirt and saw the neat row of stitches. Sam had done a good job. She was a bit surprised it wasn't covered with a bandage, but figured Sam knew what he was doing. Thank God they hadn't brought her to a hospital. She really did hate them. She thought back to the one time she'd had to spend time there and shuddered. She'd rather have Sam stitch her up any day of the week then go through that again.

Looking around, Caroline could tell she was in a hotel room, but not where or which one. She should've been freaking out, but the last thing she'd remembered was the three SEALs staring down at her tenderly as she passed out on the cot on the plane. If she couldn't trust a SEAL, then she couldn't trust anyone.

She carefully got out of bed and stumbled to the bathroom as if she was drunk. She couldn't remember the last time she'd eaten and she felt pretty weak and unsteady on her feet. Caroline used the toilet gratefully, then noticed the brand new toothbrush and toothpaste on the counter. She pounced on them and brushed her teeth thoroughly. She'd never take that for granted again.

Seeing the shower, she suddenly had an intense urge to get clean. She knew she probably shouldn't get her stitches wet, but she *had* to have that shower. She figured she'd try to keep her injured side out of the water, but if it got wet, it got wet. She could still *feel* the blood splatter from the terrorist's neck. She felt itchy and didn't want to even think about the germs she'd picked up from rolling around on the floor of the plane and then sleeping on the ground at the airport.

She tore off the shirt that she never wanted to see again, throwing it in the trash. She thought briefly about the fact that she wasn't wearing any pants. Someone, hopefully it had been Matthew, had taken them off of her before putting her to bed. The thought made her tingly inside, but she pushed it aside. He'd obviously been gentlemanly enough not to remove her shirt, and even though she didn't really know Matthew, figured he'd probably turned his head when he undid and removed her pants.

Caroline took a much quicker shower than she really wanted to, just enough to get clean and wash her hair, but she did take the time to wash her hair twice. She would've stayed in the shower all day enjoying the beat of the hot water on her back, but she had to figure out what was going on and where she was. She stepped out of the shower and wrapped herself up in a fluffy bathrobe that was on the back of the door.

She stepped back into the room and noticed for the first time her suitcase sitting on the floor. What the hell? How had that gotten here? The last thing she remembered was that the airline had said they would send all the luggage to Virginia when they were done with it. Damn. She hated not knowing what had happened. Caroline remembered being on the plane with Sam, Christopher, and Matthew, but nothing after Sam started stitching her up. That shot was definitely stronger than anything she'd ever taken before. She'd always reacted strongly to drugs, something they couldn't have known.

She sighed and sat on the side of the bed. She noticed a piece of paper on the table next to the bed and leaned over gingerly, not wanting to tweak her side, to grab it.

Caroline. If you're reading this I'm not there to tell you what's up. Don't worry, everything is fine. You were out of it when we landed yesterday. We met up with the Feds and they released your bag to us (guess there's an advantage to being a SEAL after all huh?). I brought you here since I didn't know what plans you made for when you got here.

You slept all night and I really wanted to talk to you when you finally woke up. Mozart assured me that you were fine, just sleeping. He said you'd wake up when you were ready.

We had to get to the base this morning to go over what happened on the plane. I haven't left for good though. I'll be back as soon as I can. I made sure there was some food in the hotel fridge, you're probably hungry. The coffee is all ready to go, just hit the on button.

I hope you feel better today. We'll talk when I get back from the base.

Matthew

Caroline held the note to her chest. Wow. It didn't really say anything romantic, but somehow it was the most romantic thing she'd ever been given by a man, okay, hell, it was the only note she'd been left by a man. She hadn't received any notes in high school, or in general. Matthew had been thinking about her. She glossed over in her mind the fact that he would've had to have carried her into the hotel room and concentrated instead on how he'd said he'd be back later.

She had no idea what time he'd left. She looked at the clock; it was currently eleven in the morning. She leaped up, as gracefully as she could with the stitches in her side, and fumbled through her suitcase for something appropriate to wear. She wanted to look casual, but at the same time neat and put together. Caroline finally decided on a pair of jeans and a fitted top. She usually wore T-shirts when she was at home, but she didn't want to see Matthew again in one.

She put her hair up with a barrette and went over to the kitchenette. There was a little refrigerator as well as a microwave and a little coffee pot. She checked, and yup, Matthew had filled it up with fresh grounds and water. She turned it on and set about tidying up the room.

She opened the refrigerator and saw that Matthew *had* made sure there was some food in there, it wasn't a lot, but it should take the edge off her hunger. She grabbed a yogurt and a pre-packaged strip of cheese. She ate those while she waited for the coffee to be done.

Caroline sat on the bed and sipped the coffee once it had filled the little cup. God, it tasted good. She wasn't sure what to do with herself. She generally was a very "busy" person. She didn't have a lot of down time, but since her job didn't start for a week or so and she had nowhere to go and nothing to do at the moment, she found herself actually enjoying the coffee she was drinking for once.

Done with her drink, she got up and put it on the table. She then lay back on the bed and relaxed.

Just as she was about to fall back asleep she heard

the click of the door lock being disengaged. She sat up carefully to see Matthew entering the other room of the suite. She could tell he was trying to be quiet.

"Hello," She greeted him softly.

Wolf turned around and smiled at her. Woah. His smile was lethal. His teeth were straight and when he smiled she could see the wrinkles crinkle up by his eyes. And if Caroline thought he was good looking in jeans and a shirt, he was positively deadly in his uniform.

"Hey, how do you feel?" Wolf asked with a happy glint in his eyes.

Wolf was glad to see Caroline was awake. As he'd told her in his note, he'd been worried about her. Mozart had assured him she was fine, but until he'd actually seen her awake he wasn't sure he believed him. She'd been completely knocked out when they'd arrived at the hotel.

"Pretty good, all things considered," Caroline told him. "How'd this morning go at the base?"

"Good. We wanted to keep your name out of it, but we had to tell the commander here in Norfolk your part in the whole thing."

Caroline nodded. "I figured you'd have to. It's fine. I'll talk to whomever I have to in order to help. If they think I can help prevent this from happening again, I'm happy to do it."

Somehow Wolf knew she'd say that. He smiled

broadly at her. "Everyone is really interested in who those guys were and what they wanted to accomplish. We didn't give them time to tell us where they were going. You said two of them were talking about coordinates right?"

At her nod he continued. "We don't know if they were planning on crashing into something like the terrorists did on 9/11, or if they were planning on landing the plane somewhere."

Wolf went over and sat next to Caroline on the bed. Just the fact they were both sitting on a bed together seemed very intimate. Caroline couldn't stop the blush that crept up her face.

Wolf took one finger and ran it lightly over her cheek. When she blushed further and bit her lip with her teeth, but didn't pull away, he leaned in closer. He watched her lips and when her tongue darted out to moisten them he nearly groaned. God, how could he ever have missed seeing her? Really seeing her before he got to know her.

He ran his index finger lightly over her bottom lip where she'd been biting it and had just licked. He could feel the hot wetness on his fingertip.

"I'm going to kiss you Caroline," he informed her somewhat gruffly. When she didn't say anything he growled out a warning. "If you don't want this, now's your last chance to say something."

Wolf could see the pulse in her neck beating hard. She swallowed, but didn't stop him. He leaned toward her and used the same index finger that had just been caressing her lip to lift her chin. He wanted to look into her eyes to ascertain if she really wanted this, but he couldn't tear his eyes away from her delectable mouth. Finally his lips met hers.

Her lips parted immediately to let him in. He didn't plunge into her mouth right away; instead he ran his tongue over her top lip, stopping to tease the same lip with a quick nip of his teeth. He pulled back a fraction of an inch to look at Caroline. She had her eyes shut and was clutching the front of his uniform with both hands.

He decided to stop messing around and went in again. This time when their lips met, Wolf thrust his tongue into her mouth and rejoiced when she met it with her own. They caressed each other over and over. Wolf retreated and she followed, then he pushed her tongue back and explored her mouth with his.

Finally, when Wolf knew he had to stop, not risk pushing them further than they were ready to go, he pulled back. One of his hands had made its way behind her neck and he'd been holding her against him. His other hand was low on her back. If they'd been standing or lying down he would've been pushing her pelvis into his own. Wolf took a deep breath, but didn't move his hands.

Caroline slowly opened her eyes. Holy Hell. Matthew was delicious. She'd been kissed before, but she'd never been kissed like that. Like Matthew needed her to breathe. Like she was precious. She didn't know what was different about that kiss from every other kiss she'd had in her life, but deep down she knew it *was* different.

Caroline loved the feel of Matthew's hands on her body—the hand behind her neck held her still and she could feel the heat of his hand on her back. She laid her forehead against his shoulder. Matthew didn't remove his hand from her neck, just followed her in and held her against him.

"Wow," was all Wolf could say at the moment.

"Wow indeed," he heard Caroline's muffled voice against his shoulder.

He chuckled. He felt great. Better than he had in a long time. Strangely, knowing she was just as affected as he was went a long way toward calming him down.

"What do you say we take today to sightsee?"

Caroline lifted her head from where it was resting against Matthew's chest and looked at him. "Sightsee?"

"Yeah, sightsee. You know the thing people do when they aren't working and are on vacation?"

Caroline chuckled. "Yeah, okay." If he wasn't going to talk about their kiss that was fine with her. "What is there to do around here?"

Wolf could tell she was relieved he wasn't rehashing their kiss. He'd give her time to digest it and come to terms with what happened, but he knew they'd have to discuss it sooner or later. He wanted more, a lot more.

"Well, I could give you a tour of the Naval Station, or we could go to the Norfolk Zoo, or the Botanical Gardens. If you like museums, there are several here. What are you in the mood to do and what can you physically do? I don't want you hurting yourself further."

Caroline went to sit up straighter and couldn't help but flinch as the move stretched her side and pulled at her stitches.

Of course Wolf saw. "All right, before we go, I want to check your side. Then how about I show you the base then we grab something to eat. We can then come back here and watch a movie. That way I don't have to keep asking you how you're feeling and you won't feel the need to lie to me."

Caroline laughed out loud. Crap. How could he know her that well so soon? "Sounds good."

When Matthew made no move to get up Caroline smiled and pointed out, "You'll have to let go of me if we're going to go anywhere."

Matthew leaned down and whispered, "What if I don't want to?"

Caroline didn't have anything to say, but the goose

bumps that rose on her arms were answer enough. Matthew smiled at her, took his arm from the back of her neck and ran it down her arm, kissed her hard, then stood up. He held out his hand to help Caroline up.

He didn't let go of her hand once she was standing but merely turned and led her to the bathroom. He helped her sit up on the counter, and had her hold up her shirt so he could see her side.

Wolf tried to keep his hands from wandering all over her creamy flesh, but it was difficult. She wasn't skinny, but she wasn't fat. She was...soft, and squishy, and Matthew loved it. He'd had all sorts of women, but this woman made him lose his legendary control faster than anyone ever had before.

Not able to resist, he ran the back of his hand up her side to just below her breast. At her sharp intake of breath he smiled and let his fingers trail back down to her side and her stitches. They looked good. Mozart had said to leave the wound unbandaged, as long as it wasn't bothering her.

"Does it hurt? Do we need to cover it up?"

Caroline shook her head. "It doesn't hurt. Sometimes the stitches catch on my shirt, but it doesn't hurt."

Wolf nodded, then ran his finger around the stitches one more time. He loved seeing her shiver in reaction. He reluctantly smoothed her shirt down and said, "Let's go before I decide we're better off staying here and getting to know each other better."

Wolf watched as Caroline gathered her stuff she needed for the day and they finally headed out the door.

Caroline couldn't remember a nicer day. The weather was behaving and it was beautiful outside. They'd spend the early afternoon strolling slowly around the base. Matthew pointed out important buildings and historical plaques. They'd even been able to get a guided tour of one of the huge ships. She couldn't remember what kind it was, but Caroline was fascinated at how everything worked on board. They had their own post office and kitchen and even jail on the ship.

After the tour Caroline was feeling tired. She'd had a tough forty eight hours and was still feeling the effects of the sedative. Matthew noticed, of course, and insisted they stop and grab take-out instead of eating in a restaurant.

When Caroline didn't complain about eating in, Wolf knew she was probably hurting more than she was letting on. The more time he spent with her, the more he got to know her. She'd probably fall flat on her face before admitting she was tired or hurting.

They'd come back to the hotel and spread their dinner out on the coffee table. She'd snuggled into Mathew's side after eating and they found an action adventure movie on the television to watch.

Wolf smiled down at the woman in his arms. Caroline fit perfectly against him. He couldn't remember having a date where he'd had a better time, especially when sex hadn't even been on the table. He knew they'd have to wait. She physically wasn't up for it for one, and Wolf didn't want to rush it. He loved just sitting and talking to her and getting to know her. Perhaps that was what was missing on his other dates—the connection, the getting to know each other outside the bedroom.

"Why the nickname Wolf?" Caroline murmured softly from beside him, asking the question out of the blue.

Wolf looked down. It actually sounded strange to hear his nickname coming from her mouth. He was so used to her always calling him "Matthew," in fact he preferred it.

"I'd love to tell you it came about because I'm stealthy or that I have the patience of a wolf, but alas it's nothing so manly as that."

Caroline picked her head up so she could see Matthew better. "Now I'm really interested. Go on."

"Many times in the military nicknames come from a soldier's name. Like, if my last name was Wolfgang or Wolfowitz, drill sergeants and the other guys would start calling me Wolf."

"But your last name isn't Wolfgang or Wolfowitz." Caroline said giggling, stating the obvious.

Wolf chucked Caroline under her chin. "Yeah, well

my nickname came from boot camp. It was a completely new experience for me and I was worked harder than I've ever been worked in my life. I was always hungry. Apparently every time we went in for chow I ate my food so fast I finished way before everyone else. I'd also be happy to eat anything the other guys didn't want."

Caroline sat all the way up, fully awake now. "Oh my God, don't tell me. You were *Hungry Like a Wolf*?"

Wolf laughed and grabbed Caroline so she fell back against him. He loved how she snuggled back down into him, shifting around until she was comfortable, like an animal burrowing down into their bed for the night. "I haven't thought about that old song in forever. Jesus. And actually, yes, I was always 'wolfing' down my food. The name stuck."

He loved hearing Caroline giggle. He knew she hadn't had a lot of reasons to laugh recently.

They both settled back down into watching the movie. When Wolf shifted about twenty minutes later, Caroline murmured under her breath and snuggled deeper into him. The fact that she was asleep, but still turned toward him, made his heart clench. Wolf was amazed she was such a heavy sleeper. In his line of work it didn't pay to sleep as heavily as she apparently did, so it'd been a long time since he'd seen it.

For the second night in a row, Wolf picked Caroline up and brought her to bed. He laid her down and pulled the covers up to her shoulders. He didn't dare remove her clothes. It was bad enough seeing as much of her as he had that morning while checking her stitches and the night before. He hadn't wanted her to be uncomfortable by sleeping in her pants. He'd reached under her shirt and had unbuttoned her pants. The warmth of her skin was heavenly next to his fingers. He thought about removing her shirt and pants now to help her into something more comfortable but knew if he started, he wasn't convinced he'd be able to stop, and he wasn't going to take advantage of her.

She'd just have to sleep in her jeans tonight. He wasn't strong enough to remove them again and leave her alone in the bed.

Wolf sat by the edge of the bed and simply watched Caroline sleeping. He studied her and tried to figure out what made her different from all the other women that had come before her. After a while he gave up. It was what it was and he wasn't going to analyze it anymore. He just wanted to enjoy it.

He still had a lot of time left before he had to leave for the next mission. While he wanted to visit with his friend, Tex, he wanted to spend most of his vacation time with Caroline. His priorities had shifted in a blink of an eye. Wolf didn't fight it.

He leaned down and kissed Caroline on the forehead. Wolf closed the hotel door softly and headed down the hall to the elevator. He'd meet back up with Mozart and Abe at Tex's house then come back early the next morning. He couldn't wait to spend another day with Caroline.

Chapter Eleven

CAROLINE ROLLED OVER the next morning and groaned. Shit. She'd done it again—fallen asleep— and Matthew had to put her to bed. She yawned and stretched, thinking she was such a lame date.

She got out of bed and instead of heading straight for the bathroom, Caroline checked the coffee pot…and smiled. It was set and ready to go. Matthew had obviously set it all up before he'd left last night. Caroline liked knowing he thought about her comfort that way. It had been so long since someone had done something so simple for her. She liked being taken care of. Caroline turned the switch to on and went back to the bedroom to get ready for the day.

After showering and checking her stitches—which were healing nicely—Caroline poured herself a cup of coffee and settled on the couch to watch TV. She was enjoying the free time to be lazy and not have to rush off to work. That time would come soon enough, so for now she was happy to lounge around.

Glancing around the room, Caroline did have to see about checking out of the hotel though. She figured Matthew had to be paying for it, as she certainly didn't give the front desk her credit card. She'd ask the hotel to switch to her card when she checked out; it wasn't fair for Matthew to pay for her room.

Since she rented an apartment before she left California, Caroline had planned on staying in a hotel for a few nights anyway until her stuff arrived. This hotel was just as good as any other. Figuring she had another couple of days before her furniture arrived from California, she relaxed against the couch again. Ahhhh, it felt so good to lounge around and be a bum. She didn't get to do it very much and it was a luxury now.

The phone ringing next to her startled her so badly she spilled her coffee. Crud. She rubbed at the coffee that had fallen on her jeans at the same time she leaned over to answer the phone. It had to be Matthew, she didn't know anyone else in the area.

"Hello?"

"Good morning, Caroline. How are you feeling today?"

God, if Caroline thought his voice was sexy in person, over the phone, rumbling in her ear? Panty melting. "I'm good. I'm sorry I conked out on you again last night. You're always taking me to bed." She blushed as soon as she said it. It sounded much dirtier out loud than it had in her head.

Wolf laughed. "Believe me, Ice, I love putting you to bed. I'm hoping sometime in the near future I can join you there."

Caroline was stunned into silence. Hell, she'd been thinking about how much she wanted him to join her in bed, but she didn't think he'd come right out and say it. She didn't know what to say.

"Caroline? You still there? Too soon?"

"Yes...er...no..." Shit. She was beyond flustered. She heard Matthew chuckle and tried to clarify. "Yeah, I'm still here, and...a bit...but I think I want that too." She still couldn't get over that Matthew, looking like he did, tall, dark and handsome, a man who could get any woman in his bed, seemed to want *her*.

She must have said that bit out loud because Matthew retorted, "Hell yeah I want you, Ice. You're smart, you're level headed, and I've wanted you since I shook your hand on the damn plane."

"Uh..." was all Caroline could get out. Holy. Shit.

Matthew continued as if he hadn't just blown her mind. "So, I'm coming over in an hour to get you. I thought I'd take you to meet my friend, Tex. The one I told you about on the plane? He's having a mini-get together with us, Abe, and Mozart and some of his friends here in town. I want you to meet him. It's casual, so don't dress up. Okay?"

Knowing this was a huge deal, meeting his friend, all Caroline could do is say, "Okay."

"I'll come up when I get there. See you soon, Caroline."

Caroline hung up the phone. An hour. She couldn't wait to see him again.

CAROLINE THREW HER head back and laughed unselfconsciously at Matthew's friend, Tex. His name was really John, but since he'd been from Texas when he joined the SEALs his nickname was naturally, Tex. He still had a thick southern accent and was just as brawny as all the other men standing around.

Tex had been on a mission and in a building which had been hit by an IED. The men downplayed the incident, but Caroline instinctively knew there was a lot more to it than they'd talked about.

Tex had lost his leg after several surgeries to try to repair it. He told her one day after he'd been admitted to the hospital again for a severe infection, he begged the doctors to just take it off. He figured it'd be better than dealing with the pain of infections and numerous surgeries to try to heal it, when he most likely wouldn't be able to walk on it again anyway.

Tex was hysterical, constantly saying outrageous things to make her laugh. Caroline didn't think she'd laughed so hard in all her life. Caroline liked all of Tex's friends as well, and had enjoyed hanging out with Christopher and Sam. The guys had told her to call them Abe and Mozart, but as she'd told them earlier, it felt weird to call them by their nicknames when she wasn't a part of their team. They'd argued with her about it, claiming she *was* a part of their damn team, but she'd gotten stubborn and crossed her arms and told them in no uncertain terms that she'd call them what she wanted and they could just deal. Abe and Mozart merely laughed and told her she could call them whatever she wanted, but she'd always be "Ice" to them.

Nobody talked about what Tex did now that he was medically retired from the Navy. Caroline had asked once and noticed the subject was quickly changed. She'd merely shrugged, figuring it was a secret Navy thing or he was embarrassed about it. Either way, it didn't matter as she probably wouldn't ever see him again.

Caroline tried not to feel self-conscious at the get together. There were some other women around, but she kept herself glued to Matthew's side. It was hard for her to open up, and she felt most comfortable with Matthew. He certainly wasn't complaining and was constantly touching her. He'd put his hand at her waist to steady her, brought her a plate of food once it was done, and brushed his hand against hers. Once he even kissed her on the top of her head when she was feeling bad for Tex and what he'd gone through. Caroline loved it, but she was still cautious. She'd never understand what Matthew saw in her.

After leaving Tex's house, Matthew had taken her to the Botanical Gardens. The gardens were beautiful. Caroline didn't know the name of many of the flowers, but she loved seeing the artistic way they'd been arranged and grown on the grounds. Matthew bought her a bouquet of some exotic type of flower and they'd made their way back to her hotel room.

Matthew came up with her to the room and settled them on the couch. They'd ordered room service and had eaten it enjoying each other's company and the relaxed conversation about nothing in particular.

As night fell, Caroline got more and more nervous. She couldn't help but think about what Matthew had said that morning about taking her to bed. One side of her, the hussy side, wanted it. The other more practical side, knew it was too soon.

"What are you thinking about so hard?" Wolf asked, putting his finger under her chin and lifting it so she had to look him in the eye.

"I...just...I want you." Caroline couldn't believe she'd just blurted it out like that.

"I want you too," Wolf returned without hesitation.

"It's just...well..."

"It's too soon." Wolf finished her sentence for her.

Caroline nodded. "I like you Matthew, but I don't know about this. About us. You're...you and I'm me...and you live in California and I just moved here..."

Wolf drew Caroline into his body. She felt so right there. He couldn't believe how right she felt. She had some valid points. They had a lot going against them, the least of which was that they lived on opposite sides of the country.

"Shhhh, Ice. I know this is crazy. We just met, but I'll tell you this, I've never, in all my life, felt about someone the way I feel about you. There's something about you that I'm having a hard time resisting."

He felt her nod against his chest and smiled.

"I'd love to spend my leave time with you and see if we think this thing between us can work out. I'm not going to say we won't make love, because I want that more than I can tell you, but I'll try to keep it easy for now. Okay?"

At her soft, "okay," he let out the breath he'd been holding. Wolf didn't know what he would've done if she'd disagreed with him.

"But that doesn't mean I'm not going to kiss you, hold you and touch you as much as I can while we're 'taking it slow.' I want to make sure you're good with that."

Caroline lifted her head from his chest and looked

him in the eyes. "I'm very good with that, Matthew."

He smiled and turned and stretched her out under him on the couch. Touching from their toes to chest, Wolf could feel Caroline's heart beating quickly under him. He could see her breathing increase and felt her hands grip his shirt at his waist.

Wolf leaned down, brought his lips low until they remained a breath above hers, and waited. She didn't disappoint him. She stretched her neck up until she could reach his mouth. He sighed in contentment. Caroline wanted the same thing he did. Thank God. It was important to him that she come to him. While he wasn't shy or usually all that concerned about being the aggressor in a relationship, with Caroline, he wanted her to be sure. He wanted her to want him as much as he wanted her.

While his lips caressed hers, his hands roamed her body gently. He kept his hands on top of her clothes, knowing he wouldn't be able to stop himself if he felt Caroline's creamy skin against his hands. Wolf was careful not to touch her injured side, but otherwise he didn't hold his roaming hands back.

He skimmed his hands over her breasts lightly, feeling her nipples peak under his touch. He kept moving, gentling her when she bucked under him and holding her tight against him so she could feel how excited he was. Wolf didn't want her to think she was alone in what she was feeling, alone in her attraction.

Finally with one hand at her hip holding her close and one hand lying over her heart, he pulled his lips away from hers reluctantly.

"Jesus, Caroline. You're perfect. Perfect for me."

As he expected, she blushed a rosy pink.

"You're not so bad yourself, Matthew."

He smiled and pulled them upright. Caroline's hair was mussed and her lips were swollen from their passionate kisses. She looked amazing. Wolf fitted her body next to his and kissed her on top of her head.

"Snuggle in, Ice. I don't want to leave yet, but we have to stop...that...so we'll watch a movie. Sound good?"

Caroline smiled. Hell yeah it sounded good.

WOLF JERKED AWAKE. He could go from asleep to being one hundred percent awake, thanks to being a SEAL. He didn't know what had woken him up until he heard a whimper. Caroline was jerking in his arms. It was obvious she was having a nightmare.

"Wake up, Ice." Wolf tried to talk her out of her dream, but Caroline just whimpered louder at his words. "Caroline." Wolf said loudly and firmly. "Wake up. You're dreaming."

Wolf wasn't ready for her reaction. She fought

against him as if she was back on the plane fighting the terrorist.

Caroline fought with all her might. The terrorist was going to hurt Matthew, she had to make sure he didn't get to him. It was up to her to save Matthew. She batted at the hands that were grabbing at her, ignoring his words. She had to fight, if she didn't, he'd kill her.

Her struggles had made them tumble off the couch—luckily he'd hit the floor first and prevented Caroline from landing on her back. Wolf's heart hurt at the expression on her face. She was terrified and his hold on her wasn't helping.

"Caroline!" Wolf yelled. She stilled, he was getting to her. He turned her over so she was lying on her back on the floor. He hovered over her, not putting his weight on her, but close enough he could still feel her body heat. "Wake up! You're safe, you're fine. You're here in Virginia, not on the plane. Come back to me. It's Matthew."

"Matthew?" Caroline's voice was soft, disbelieving.

"Yes, open your eyes."

Caroline forced her eyes to open and saw that it was, indeed, Matthew. He was straddled over her, leaning down peering into her eyes intently.

"Oh shit," Caroline whispered.

"Come on, let's get you up off the floor." Wolf helped her sit up and situated back on the couch. As soon as she was, he sat next to her and pulled her into his chest.

"You're okay. It was just a dream."

Caroline shook with the aftereffects of the images that had been flitting through her head. It had seemed so real.

"Want to talk about it?"

She shook her head against his chest, not looking up.

"Okay. I'm assuming it was about what happened on the plane?" At her nod he told her, "You need to talk to someone about it, Caroline. If you don't, the dreams won't stop. Believe me, I know."

At that, Caroline looked up at Matthew. "You know?"

He looked grim, but met her eyes. "Yeah, in my line of work there's no way I can keep it all bottled in. It's true most men in the military don't like to admit to weaknesses when it comes to nightmares and PTSD, but we're required to debrief anytime we have a heavy mission. In fact, Abe, Mozart, and I are required to meet with someone here to talk about what happened on the plane."

Caroline could only stare up at him in amazement. "Really?"

Wolf chuckled and brought her into his chest again. She tucked her head under his chin and wrapped her arms around his waist. He changed position until he was lying with his head on the armrest of the couch, shifting Caroline until she was lying with her front settled along his side. Her arm came to rest on his chest, where she idly drew shapes over his heart.

"Yeah. Can't say I like all the shrinks they make us see, but honestly, it works. We might grumble about it, but if it keeps us sane, and ready for our next mission, we'll do it."

"I was fighting that guy. I knew if he got the better of me or if I let him go, he'd go and kill you. I didn't want you to die." Caroline spoke quietly and from the heart.

"Oh, sweetheart." Wolf tightened his arms around her. "You were so brave. I'm so proud of you. But..." he waited until she raised her eyes to his. When she was looking at him, he continued. "I can take care of myself. Don't ever put yourself in danger again for me. Promise me."

"But Matthew, this is just...I don't..." Shit. She'd never had a hard time expressing what she wanted to say before. But the right words just wouldn't come to her.

He shook his head. "No buts. Just promise me Caroline. Look after you first. Always."

She could only nod. The look in his eyes was intense. She broke eye contact and laid her head back down. She gripped him harder and brought the hand that was lying on his chest up and curled it around the back of his neck and squeezed.

"Sleep now. I'm here. I'll make sure nothing happens to you."

"Thank you. I feel safe here with you."

Caroline fell asleep still clutching him. Wolf had never felt more content in all his life. Usually he felt antsy sleeping with a woman; never letting her cuddle into him, and leaving as soon as it was socially acceptable. But with Caroline all bets were off.

Long after the sun fell from the sky Wolf eased out from under her. He once more carried Caroline to bed. He laughed quietly to himself. This was becoming a habit for him—one he liked.

As he spread the comforter over Caroline, Wolf heard the shrill ring of his phone in the other room in the suite. Crap. His phone didn't ring unless it was work. No! They still had over a week before they were supposed to leave. Maybe it was about the terrorist incident? With one final look at Caroline and one last light kiss to her forehead, Wolf closed the bedroom door softly and went to answer his phone, hoping against hope it was nothing important.

CAROLINE STRETCHED CAREFULLY as she woke, amazed at how quickly her side was healing, and looked around.

Crap. Really? Third time in a row? Once again she didn't remember how she'd gotten to bed. She *did* remember her nightmare and the intense make out session with Matthew though.

Smiling at the memory, Caroline immediately looked at the pillow next to her and saw a piece of paper folded up.

Her heart raced and she couldn't wait to see what he had to say. Caroline reached over and grabbed the unassuming little note and opened it.

Caroline, you have to know I hate having to write you another note. Hopefully one day I can be right there next to you when you wake up...Now that you're blushing...

Jesus, this man knew her so well. Caroline kept reading.

...You know Mozart, Abe, and I came out here to Norfolk for vacation before our mission started; unfortunately that mission came sooner than we thought it would. I've had a great time spending time with you over the last couple of days. If it's okay, I'd like to get in touch with you when we get back. I'd like to get to know you better. I know we have some things to work out, mainly the distance between our homes, but I still want to explore what's happening between us. I'm not sure how

long it'll take for us to get back to Norfolk. Sometimes our missions are short, but other times they can drag on much longer than we'd like. I'm leaving my cell phone number so you can call me. If you'd like to get together when I get back (and I hope you will!) just call and leave me a number where I can reach you. I'll call as soon as we get back. Good luck with your new job. Knock 'em dead! Matthew. PS. Abe and Mozart say hello and they're sorry they didn't get to hang out with us last night. I didn't tell them I wasn't…

Caroline read the letter twice and hugged it to her chest. She wasn't sure what to do about Matthew. It was a heady feeling, one she'd never experienced. No one ever wanted to get to know her better. It was almost too good to be true.

Caroline carefully put the letter in her purse and took a deep breath. Time to get back to her real life. She wasn't a SEAL and needed to contact her employer to let him know what was going on. She could even start work early if he wanted her to and she almost hoped he did. She needed something to take her mind off of Matthew and everything that had happened recently.

Caroline packed up and took one last look around the hotel room on her way out. She was headed to the apartment she'd rented before coming out to Virginia. Before she left, she pulled out both letters Matthew had left her and read them one more time. On impulse she added his number to her cell phone contacts. Not that she was going to call him…they couldn't possibly work out…it was better to end things now before she fell in love with him…wasn't it?

Chapter Twelve

Two weeks later.

F OR THE MOST part, Caroline was enjoying her job. It was much the same as she'd done in San Diego. A chemist's work really wasn't that exciting to most people no matter where it was done, but Caroline loved it. It was hard to explain to someone else why or even what she did. She was just fascinated how the mixing of chemicals could make something useful and lifesaving, or it could make it destructive and deadly. She recalled how Matthew had seemed interested when she'd tried to explain what it was she did to him.

She'd actually dialed Matthew's cell phone a few times in the last few days. Each time she planned to leave a message agreeing to see him when he got back, but she chickened out each time. Heck she had no idea if he was even back already. What if he'd changed his mind and decided a relationship was too much trouble? Did he even want a relationship? She was driving herself nuts.

Caroline decided to give Matthew the benefit of the doubt and believe he was still out of the country. So she'd called him. Just hearing his voice on his voice mail was enough to snap her to her senses. What was she doing? They had a great time in those couple of days together, but what if he was just feeling grateful she'd help save his life, or he was just concerned about her in the way someone would be concerned about a sister?

Of course the kisses they shared didn't *feel* like a brother/sister kiss to her. She sighed. She usually wasn't this indecisive. When she wanted something she went for it. But then again, she'd never had someone who looked like Matthew show her any attention before.

Caroline thought about the three SEALs quite a bit over the last two weeks. She supposed you didn't go through something like what they had and not feel some sort of connection. She did want to know if Matthew, Sam, and Christopher were all okay and back safe from wherever they'd gone, but she was embarrassed to actually leave him a message. Matthew was the kind of man a woman only dreamed about. He was the type of man that tall gorgeous women dated, not someone like her; a geeky scientist.

The media had been going crazy over the hijacking. Every time she turned on the TV a story about it was on. Caroline had seen Brandy all over the various news channels. Brandy had no idea what she was talking about, as she'd hidden in the back of the plane while everything was happening, but the news outlets were still clamoring to talk to her.

There was a lot of talk about the "mysterious" men who'd saved the day, but from what Caroline had seen, so far no one knew who they were. And there had been no mention of her name that she could tell, thank God.

One thing Caroline did hear when she'd watched one of the stories that made her extremely nervous, was when the hijacking was called a "trial run" for a bigger operation of taking over planes that was supposed to have happened later on. *That* had certainly riled the country up. Airline security had been tightened, and people were obviously scared to fly. But what made Caroline nervous was knowing it wasn't just four people acting alone. There was someone, or some *people* out there who wanted to do it again and possibly hurt and kill more innocent people. Caroline wouldn't wish what she'd gone through on anyone else.

After seeing that news story Caroline had tried to not watch anything else on the hijacking. She'd lived it, and knew the truth, and honestly it was just freaking her out hearing all the political reasons why it might have happened. She started listening to the oldies radio station for noise factor instead of turning on the television.

Caroline's new apartment wasn't too far from where

she worked, so she didn't need to drive to get there. She took the bus most places she had to go, but Caroline would drive to the beach or up the coast. She enjoyed the Virginia countryside. It was soothing to her frazzled nerves.

As far as getting to work, Caroline varied her travel times and routes, any single woman alone knew it was a smart thing to do, but she still felt extraordinarily nervous. A few times she'd thought she was being followed, but when she tried to figure out by whom, she couldn't find anyone who looked suspicious. Caroline had also been getting hang up calls at work—answering the phone to no one there, or at least they weren't saying anything.

Caroline hadn't given much thought to the episodes before she'd seen the news reports about the attempted hijacking she'd been involved with. With the potential threat for other planned hijackings, now she couldn't *not* think about them! What if somehow the terrorist group, knew who she was and about her part in the failed hijacking? What if they were following her?

A few days after watching the news reports about the hijacking, Caroline was late leaving the office—working late on a project that was having a breakthrough. Her coworkers had stayed as well, but they'd all left in their cars to head home. Caroline actually watched them walk to their cars, leaving her standing in the doorway of the office building. She mentally shook her head. She was the only one who used public transportation and no one thought to ask if she wanted a ride home. Too independent for her own good sometimes, Caroline knew she should've just asked for a ride—now it was too late.

Caroline wistfully thought about Matthew. She knew he was the type of man that would never let a woman take any type of public transportation this late at night alone. At the very least he'd escort her home. She sighed. Caroline never thought about this sort of thing until she'd met Matthew and his team. She'd just taken it as status quo and gone about her business.

Caroline got out her cell phone and walked with a purpose toward the bus stop. She only had to go three blocks, but it was dark out. Luckily the bus arrived not too much after she arrived at the bus stop, which was good because Caroline didn't want to stand in the dark waiting for it. She was too freaked out.

The feeling she was being watched didn't abate once she was on the bus. Once again she didn't see any passengers that looked out of place, but she couldn't get rid of the creepy feeling.

She hurried off at her stop and power walked all the way to her apartment building. She didn't relax until she'd made it inside and had closed and locked the door. Keeping her phone in her hand so she could beat herself up over whether or not to call Matthew later that night, she put her purse and bag down and headed toward the bathroom. She wanted to splash some cold water on her face and change out of her work clothes. The anxiety about her uncertain relationship with Matthew, her feelings of being watched, along with the stress of the aftermath of the hijacking were messing with her big time. She wasn't sleeping well and she was exhausted.

As she reached the bathroom, she heard a noise behind her. She looked back and saw the doorknob of her apartment being turned. The door was locked, but someone was out there. Holy crap. She wasn't losing her mind. Someone *had* to have been following her. If it was someone who wanted to talk to her legitimately they would've knocked. No one came up to a door and grabbed the doorknob to open it; they knocked and announced themselves...unless they were up to no good.

Caroline didn't wait to see who was at the door, or if they got through it or not. She bolted into the bedroom and opened the window at the fire escape. She had no idea if it would trick the person at the door into believing she'd left that way or not, but maybe, just maybe they'd think she fled and wouldn't take the time to search the rest of the apartment.

She raced back toward the bathroom just as she heard the creak of the front door notifying her that someone had just opened it. They'd obviously used some sort of lock pick to get in; otherwise she would've heard the door being broken down. They were trying to sneak up on her to surprise her. They also obviously didn't want to make a ruckus so others in the complex would hear and become suspicious.

Heart racing, she entered the bathroom and left the door open. She prayed the open bedroom window would make whoever it was think that she left that way. The open bathroom door would hopefully also make them think no one was in there. She climbed into the tub and eased the shower curtain most of the way shut. She didn't close it all the way, again in the hopes that it would look like no one was in the shower.

Caroline noticed her cell phone in her hand. Thank God. She almost cried in relief. She quickly dialed 911 and waited for someone to answer.

"Hello, 911, what is your emergency?"

Caroline heard the voice on the other end of the phone and literally sagged in relief. She had no idea who the person was, or what they looked like, and she didn't really care. All she cared about was that someone was there to help her.

Whispering in a voice so low she had no idea if the woman on the other end of the line could hear her, she said, "I'm in my apartment, someone broke in. I'm hiding in the shower. Please. Hurry!"

"Okay, I've got your address. The police are on the

way. Stay put, stay quiet, they'll be there as soon as they can."

Caroline sighed in relief. The 911 operator's voice was calm and soothing, just what she needed at that moment. Still whispering Caroline said, "Thank you," then hit the off button on the phone. She knew she probably was supposed to stay on the line until the cops got there, but she couldn't, she wanted to hear Matthew's voice.

Caroline hit his name in her address book and dialed his cell, almost on autopilot. She didn't know who was in her house, but whoever it was, wasn't going to let her live if they were somehow related to the terrorist incident. She knew it.

Caroline didn't want Matthew thinking she never wanted to see him again. If he got back from his mission and didn't hear from her that's exactly what he'd think. He'd probably never know she'd been thinking about him and how much she'd enjoyed the time they'd spent together. It was time to leave that message for him.

She waited through his message, tearing up at hearing his low, grumbly voice. After the beep she whispered, *"Hi Matthew, it's me, Caroline...um...Ice. I wanted to let you know I would've loved to have gotten together with you again when you got back. I didn't want you to think that I didn't....but I don't know if I'll be here.....I'm in my apartment, but someone just broke in. I'm hiding in the bathroom. I've called 911, but if they don't get here in time... I wanted you to know that I desperately wanted to see you again..."*

Caroline hit the disconnect button to end the call and turned off the phone entirely. She didn't want the concerned sounding emergency operator calling her back and having the phone ring at the wrong time. Even on vibration mode, the ringing could still be heard.

She tried to slow her breaths and be as quiet as she could. That was harder than she thought. It was scary that she was actually hoping it was just someone that wanted to rob her, or God forbid assault her, but deep down she knew whoever it was would kill her if he found her. She listened as whoever it was in her apartment went into her bedroom and closed her window. Caroline thought she heard him swear, then she heard him going through her drawers. She couldn't even be embarrassed. He could look at her undies all he wanted, if he just *left*.

At one point, he actually came into the bathroom, looked through her medicine cabinet and even used the toilet. Caroline was afraid to breathe. She was more scared now than she was on the plane. All it would take is one breath, one wrong movement, one cough, one sneeze, to alert him she was there. Matthew and his team weren't there to help her. Caroline was on her own and she suddenly realized how out of her element she really was. She thought she was brave, but when push came to shove, she realized she wasn't brave at all. She'd never felt so alone in all her life.

Finally whoever it was left the bathroom. Caroline heard sirens in the distance, running feet and her door close quietly. Jesus, he didn't even slam the damn door. That said a lot about his control and level of professionalism. She didn't move. What if there were two of them in her apartment? What if the person wasn't really gone and only wanted her to *think* he left the apartment to try to draw her out.

Caroline stood silent and quiet even when she heard the police banging on her front door. She was frozen in fear, but desperately wanted to rush to the door and throw herself into the officers' arms. But the more she thought about it, the more she realized she couldn't trust even the police, what if it wasn't really the cops? She didn't move until she heard the officers in her little apartment. Knowing she couldn't stay cowering in her shower forever, she slowly moved the curtain aside and called out to the officers.

Chapter Thirteen

W OLF COULDN'T WAIT until the ship he was on got closer to land. He wanted to check his voice mail, but knew it wouldn't work until they were in range of a cell phone tower on American soil. For the thousandth time he wished he had a satellite phone, but of course that was impractical for everyday use. He shook his head and laughed at himself. He was worse than a high schooler with his first crush.

Mozart and Abe had given him a hard time, but he knew they were just as anxious to hear from Caroline, to make sure she was all right. They'd really taken to her and had told Wolf all the time how lucky he was.

Cookie, Benny, and Dude hadn't met Caroline, but they'd certainly heard all about her from the team. They'd been stunned at her actions on the plane and had asked a million questions about her job as a chemist. Wolf knew they'd find her as amazing as he did. As long as they kept their hands to themselves, all would be well.

Wolf should've been surprised at how possessive he felt about Caroline, but he wasn't. It just seemed right. He couldn't be freaked out about it when she felt like *his*.

It went against everything Wolf knew to leave Caroline in that hotel bed without talking to her first, but he didn't have a choice. As soon as he'd answered his phone he knew he'd have to leave. His boss had notified Wolf the situation had changed and they had to go right away. No one argued with him, such was life as a Navy SEAL, but Wolf hadn't liked it. For the first time in his life there was someone in his life that came before his job.

Being a Navy SEAL had always come first. Always. At no time had he allowed a woman to dictate what he did when. It felt weird because in the past when a woman tried to tie him down, he got antsy and broke things off. Now, he *wanted* Caroline to tie him down. He didn't know if he loved her, but he figured with the way he felt about her after the short time he'd spent with her, he was well on his way.

When he'd made it to the ship Mozart and Abe wanted to know how Caroline was doing. How was her side? Were the stitches okay? Wolf had answered their questions and told them how much he'd enjoyed his time with her. Expecting the guys to give him crap, he was shocked when they'd just smiled at him and told him it was about time he found a woman who was good enough for him.

Even Tex had pulled him aside at his house and told him how much he liked Caroline. Tex had always been an easy-going guy and never, not once, had he commented on Wolf's choice of woman...until Caroline. His team's approval meant a lot to him. That wasn't to say Wolf would've listened to them if they didn't like her, but he was glad they did. They'd hopefully be seeing more of Caroline in the future.

Finally the phone in Wolf's hand vibrated. They'd sailed close enough to the United States to be able to receive a signal. Thank God he had a message! He eagerly drew the phone up to his ear, hoping to hear Caroline's voice saying she wanted to see him again.

"Hi Matthew, it's me, Caroline...um...Ice..." At first Wolf was thrilled to hear her voice, but confused about why she was whispering. Then his blood ran cold. *What the hell? Oh shit.* His Caroline was in trouble. Listening to her soft voice quavering in fear was heart wrenching. She'd been in trouble and called to reassure *him*. Jesus. She knew he couldn't help her, but she'd called anyway. Wolf couldn't even think. *Him*, the Navy SEAL, had no idea what to do.

He spun, took the stairs two at a time, and burst into the day room. All five members of his team looked up sharply, instantly alarmed. They'd never seen Wolf so frazzled and it put them on high alert.

"Caroline," was all he could get out. He was breathing hard and was definitely panicked. Mozart and Abe came over to him and Wolf just held out the phone. Abe grabbed it and played the message on the speaker for them all to hear.

No one said a word until Mozart uttered, "Fuck." It looked like she'd called about twenty-four hours ago. Twenty-four freaking hours ago. There were no other messages from her. No one wanted to say it, but they all knew that wasn't a good sign.

They couldn't get off the ship for at *least* another four hours. They had to dock and get clearance. Benny, Cookie, and Dude hadn't met Caroline, but with everything they'd heard enough about her from the others, they were just as concerned about her as Mozart, Abe, and Wolf were. Well, maybe not as concerned as Wolf.

Wolf immediately dialed the number Caroline had called from. He listened to it ring and ring and ring. When her message came on, he didn't bother to listen to it. As much as he wanted to hear her voice again, he wanted to hear her in person, not a recording. He hung up and called back. He had no idea how many times he would've kept calling her back, probably until one of his team members confiscated his phone, but luckily the third time he'd hit her number she finally answered.

"Hello?" She answered tentatively.

"Caroline?" Wolf said urgently, hoping like hell it was her. How she'd become so important to him in such a short time, he had no idea. But there it was. It was the moment he'd heard her whispered voice and realized he wasn't there and couldn't help her that he knew she was his. Period. His.

"Yes, this is she," Caroline said shakily. She hadn't recovered from the break in at her apartment and didn't recognize the voice on the other end of the line.

"It's me, Wolf...er...Matthew. Are you okay? Jesus, Caroline. Talk to me."

"Matthew!" Caroline breathed a sigh of relief. Oh my God, she was so relieved to hear his voice she had to sit down. She collapsed on a chair that luckily was nearby, then remembered the message she'd left for him. "Are you back? Are you calling to see when we can get together?" Caroline tried to play dumb and pretend Matthew was calling about a date. Maybe he hadn't checked his voice mail yet. She wasn't thinking straight because he wouldn't know her number if he hadn't checked his messages. She also knew by the tone of his voice when he'd asked if she was all right, he'd heard the panicked message she'd left.

"What the hell, Caroline?" He practically roared at her. "Are you all right woman? What the hell is going on?"

Caroline winced. Shit. Maybe she shouldn't have called him from her apartment after all. He sounded pissed, not excited to hear from her. She leaned over in the chair clutching her stomach. Her lower lip trembled and she closed her eyes.

Abe grabbed the phone from Wolf and glared at him as he brought it up to his ear. Abe knew Wolf was frantic, but Jesus, he was going to piss Ice off or scare her away if he didn't get control of himself.

"This is Abe, Ice. What Wolf *meant* to say was that he got your message and he wanted to make sure you were all right," he said quietly gesturing at Wolf to "relax" and shooting daggers at him with his eyes.

Caroline sighed and choked back a sob. "I'm okay, Christopher. Thanks. Can you put Matthew back on? Please?" Caroline was impressed she remembered his real name. She'd been afraid she'd forget them, so she'd repeated them to herself several times over the last few weeks, making sure she knew them backward and forward.

Abe looked over at his team leader. Wolf was sitting on a chair with his head resting on his clenched fists. He could see the whites of Wolf's knuckles and could tell he was in no condition to talk rationally yet.

"Um, no, sorry, not just yet. Why don't you tell me what's going on."

Caroline sighed. Christopher had asked her to tell

him what was going on, but she knew it wasn't really a question. It was a demand.

"I didn't mean to upset him, Christopher. God, can you tell him that? I just...hell...If something happened, I didn't want Matthew to think I didn't want to see him again. That's all. He's the best thing that's happened to me in my life." She paused, took a deep breath, and continued. "Then I ...got busy...and forgot to call him back." That was a lie, but she figured it was safer for the moment to stretch the truth. She didn't want to blurt out that she missed Matthew terribly and had wanted to call him every day, every hour. That was a little too "stalkerish," even for her.

Abe repeated his question. "What's going on? I can tell you aren't telling me everything. You *know* I hate it when people lie. Tell me, Ice. Tell me now."

Caroline didn't like the hardness in Christopher's voice, but she knew she wouldn't be able to beat around the bush for much longer. She told him a watered down version of what had happened at her apartment.

"I got home from work and someone tried to break in. I hid in the bathroom until the cops got there and whoever it was left."

Abe knew there was more to what happened than what she'd told him. Hell, she'd tried to downplay wrestling with a damn terrorist; there was no way that two sentence explanation was anywhere *close* to what had happened. Deciding to let it rest until they could see her in person, he informed her, "It'll take us a bit to get over there, probably about five hours or so, but don't you *move* from your apartment until we get there. Okay?"

Caroline hesitated.

"Okay, Ice?" Abe asked again impatiently when she didn't immediately agree.

"I'm not at my apartment, Christopher." Caroline told him in a small voice.

"Where the hell are you then?" Abe practically shouted at her.

Caroline flinched at the other end of the phone as she sat up in the chair. Her stomach hurt. This was horrible. She wanted Matthew and his team there, but she wanted them to be safe more. Why were they yelling at her? Crap. She drew her feet up and sat them on the chair by her butt. She grabbed her knees with one arm and held the phone to her ear with the other hand. She couldn't deal with this on top of everything else. A new voice came on the other end of the phone.

Dude had taken the phone from Abe. "Ice? My name's Dude and I'm on Wolf's team. I take it you aren't at home? Why don't you tell me where you are and we can come and see in person that you're okay."

Caroline shook her head. "Sorry Faulkner, it *is* Faulkner right? I'm trying to match up everyone's given names with nicknames. Matthew told me all about you guys, and I think I have it, but I could make a mistake." Caroline knew she was stalling so she continued, "I don't really know you though. I'm not telling someone I haven't met where I am, even if you *are* in the same room as Matthew and Christopher."

Silence followed her pronouncement, and yet another voice came at her from the other end of the phone.

"Ice, this is Mozart. You remember me right?"

Caroline snorted, and it came out as a half laugh and half sob. It looked they were going to keep passing the phone around until everyone on the team spoke with her. "Duh. Of course I do. You did such a pretty embroidery job on my side, Sam." She tried to keep it light.

"That's right. Now where are you?" Mozart cut to the chase, glad to hear her voice and know she seemed to be okay, but not happy at the way she was prevaricating. "Why aren't you at your apartment?"

"It's a long story, Sam, but I can't tell you right now."

"Why not, Ice? Please, you know you can trust us, we'll help you."

"I know, but I'm not allo.....I just can't. Okay?"

"Allowed? You aren't allowed to tell us? What the *hell,* Ice?" Mozart sputtered, getting more and more incensed and worried about her.

Wolf finally had himself under control and gestured for his phone back. Mozart saw that Wolf did indeed seem to have himself back under his iron control and handed the phone over while whispering urgently, "Find out what the hell's going on and do it now. Something's wrong."

Wolf nodded curtly and tried to soften his tone when he spoke into the phone again. "Caroline? It's Matthew."

"I know," Caroline told him softly, "I recognize your voice now."

"I need to know where you are, honey," Wolf pleaded, emotion coating his words, "Please."

"Matthew, I'm not allowed to tell anyone. I'm not even supposed to be on the phone."

Ignoring the "allowed" comment for the moment, Wolf tried to back up a bit. She'd get to it; he just had to make her feel safe with him again. In a tender voice, he urged, "Tell us what happened Caroline. Please. I'm going to put you on speaker so we can all hear you and you don't have to repeat it."

Caroline sighed. When Matthew spoke to her in that low urgent voice she really couldn't deny him anything. She wasn't happy about being on speaker, and having his entire team hear what had happened, but Matthew had a good point. She didn't want to repeat her story a million times either.

"It was dark when I headed home from work and all the way home I felt like someone was watching me. Actually I felt that way all week."

Before she could continue, Wolf interrupted her. "Why'd you leave work so late? Why didn't anyone make sure you got home all right?"

Caroline hesitated; she didn't want Faulkner, Hunter, or Kason to have to hear about how she was. "Matthew, I *told* you about me already. You *know*."

Wolf gritted his teeth. Dammit.

Abe broke in before Wolf could say anything. "Caroline, it's Abe. We might not have noticed you in the airport before we knew you, but any man who's any kind of man would've made sure you got home all right."

Caroline shook her head. They just didn't understand. They were *there*. They'd seen the men on the plane leave with the pretty women and ignore her when she'd decided to stay at the airport. Hell, *they'd* left her there too. She willed the tears back. Now wasn't the time. She had to get through this story.

"Anyway, so I felt like someone was following me, but I didn't see anyone. When I got home, I heard someone at my door trying to get in. I opened the bedroom window that leads to the fire escape in the hopes whoever it was would think I heard him and went out that way. I then hid inside the shower in the bathroom and called 911. The lady that answered was so nice. She kept calm and tried to make sure *I* was calm."

Wolf could hear the way her voice wobbled as she'd talked about calling for help while hiding in her damn shower. "You called me too," he murmured in a low voice.

Forgetting she was on speaker and all of his team could hear her, she admitted, "Yeah. All I could think of is that if you'd been there, I'd have felt so much safer and you would've taken care of it…me."

Jesus. Wolf tried to reassure her. He could hear in the tone of her voice how scared she'd been. "I'm sorry I wasn't there. You're right, I would've taken care of you." After letting that sink in he urged her to continue. "Go on, tell us the rest."

"Well, the police came and I told them what happened. The next thing I knew the FBI was there talking to me, telling me I had to go to a safe house." She lowered her voice, "I don't understand what's going on, Matthew. The FBI wouldn't really say why they thought I had to be put here. I don't know who to trust and I don't know what's going on. I don't think it had to do with the plane, but even if it did, I didn't tell the FBI anything. I swear I didn't, Matthew."

"Shhh, I know you didn't, hon. I promise we'll figure this out. You trust us right? You trust me?"

"I do, Matthew. Out of everyone throughout this I trust you and Christopher and Sam."

"Caroline, you can trust Benny, Cookie, and Dude too. Don't trust anyone else but my team. No one. Understand?"

Caroline nodded, then remembering that he couldn't see her, said, "Yeah, I understand. But I've never met your teammates, so I don't know what they look like. How can I trust them if I wouldn't know them on the street if I saw them?"

Wolf hadn't thought of that. Abe spoke up.

"Ice, remember the code you used to let me know on the plane that something was wrong?"

Caroline had forgotten Christopher and the others could hear her conversation with Matthew.

"Yes," she told him slowly.

"When you meet any of our team, we'll use that signal in our handshake to you. So if someone says they're Dude or Cookie or Benny, and you shake their hand and they don't give you the signal, you'll know it's not really them. Understand?"

"Okay, but is this really all necessary? You're scaring me." She said in a soft voice. "I'm just a chemist. Why me? I'm not cut out for any of this."

Cookie cut in. "Ice, this is Cookie, first of all, thank you for saving my team's sorry butts on the plane that day. And I understand why you're having trust issues and that's okay for now. But know while you're deciding on whether or not you can trust us, we'll be figuring out what's going on and we'll keep you safe. Okay?"

Caroline took a deep breath. "Okay, but *you* guys stay safe. I don't know what's going on, but you'd better not get hurt or caught up in whatever this is. I'm sure the FBI has it under control…Oh…someone's coming. I have to go."

Before she could hang up Wolf said softly. "We're coming for you, Ice. Stay strong." The phone connection was cut.

Wolf's team sat there for a moment looking at each other.

Finally Cookie said, "We'll figure this out, Wolf. We'll keep your woman safe. We'll stake our lives on it."

"I'm counting on it Cookie. I'm counting on it," Wolf responded softly, realizing again what his team already knew. Caroline was his. And he'd protect what was his. His team would protect her too. All because she was Wolf's.

Chapter Fourteen

C AROLINE SAT IN the room in the little cabin not sure what was really going on. She'd talked to one of the FBI agents who was guarding her. He hadn't told her much, but it was enough for her to make some deductions.

Apparently the hijacking attempt *was* part of a larger terrorist plan. The fact it hadn't succeeded and airline security was heightened pissed off the terrorists and now they were after her. She wasn't clear on how they even *knew* she was on the plane, nonetheless what had happened since all four of the terrorists on the plane were dead. That was the scariest part. Someone knew, and that person had passed her name along to terrorists. *Terrorists* for God's sake.

Caroline felt as if she was in a movie. These things just didn't happen to people like her. She was painfully ordinary. She wasn't brave, she wasn't a hero, she wasn't cut out for this.

She worried about her job. She'd just started and

now they were saying she couldn't go back to it until they caught whoever was behind the threats and caught the people who were after her. Jesus, that could be any number of people. Caroline hated to think she might have to give up her profession, her job and be stuffed away into the Witness Protection Program. She had no idea what her new boss thought. He'd probably written her off by now and was looking into hiring someone new.

The worst thought about having to go into the Witness Protection Program was losing Matthew. She was just getting to know him. She wasn't naïve enough to think they'd end up married or anything, they'd only started seeing each other and getting to know each other, but the thought of leaving and never getting the chance to get to know him better was depressing. Figures, just when she found the sexiest man she'd ever seen, and he seemed interested in her, she'd have to disappear forever.

She sighed. She couldn't even *talk* to Matthew because the FBI agent caught her when she hung up with Matthew and his team and took her phone away. The FBI agent had been mad, but she was mad too. It wasn't fair. What was she supposed to *do* in this stupid cabin? Why couldn't she talk to anyone? How many times had people been brought to cabins for their safety only to die because someone snuck up on it? She didn't know if she'd feel any safer in the city in an apartment, but out here she felt exposed.

She'd heard the phone ring a few times while she was in her room, but ignored it. It was the FBI agent's phone. Caroline stayed on her bed. She wasn't sleeping, but she was so tired. She wanted nothing more than to be able to fall into a dreamless sleep, but every time she closed her eyes, she relived the hijacking and had other dreams about faceless enemies shooting at her and trying to kill her. She hadn't had the nightmares since she'd been with Matthew in the hotel, but after the break-in they'd returned with a vengeance.

It had been a couple of days since she'd spoken with Matthew and his team. When she'd talked to him, he'd said it'd take about five hours to get to her apartment, but she hadn't told them where she was now. She wouldn't, even if she knew exactly where she was. If anything happened to them because of her, she'd never forgive herself. Caroline didn't know what was going on, but she certainly didn't want to bring anyone else into it. And besides, she tried to tell herself, they'd just gotten back from a mission and needed their rest too. She was on her own, just as she'd always been.

Caroline didn't know how long she'd been sitting on her bed zoning out when she heard voices in the other room. She didn't get up. It was just the agents switching out. She waited for one to knock on the door, introduce himself and to check on her. It'd been what had happened every other time someone new had come. When she continued to hear the voices she went to her door and opened it. She was shocked. Matthew! What was he doing here? How had he found her? What was going on?

Wolf smiled at Caroline. She looked great...well, not really. She looked tired and stressed, but he was so very glad to see her. He turned back to the agent. It'd taken his team a while, with Tex's help, to track Caroline down, and none of them liked what they'd found out in the process.

Wolf had talked to their commander back in San Diego, and convinced him there was something big going down and that he and his team needed to be here. His commander agreed there was a leak somewhere, in the FBI most likely, and promised he'd look into it discretely.

His commander told Wolf their actions wouldn't be sanctioned by the Navy, but he'd do what he could to keep the heat off of them. He also allowed them to stay in Virginia and unofficially officially work the case. He'd greased some wheels with people he knew in both the FBI and the Navy, and they were now officially working together.

There was a double agent in the FBI. That was the only thing that made sense. Someone had leaked information back to the terrorist organization about what had happened on that plane, and had told them Caroline had a role in the failure of the mission. As a result, Caroline had a bounty on her head. The terrorists wanted her dead. They figured if they couldn't reach the SEALs responsible, they'd kill Caroline. Wolf was furious. Unknowingly he'd been responsible for her being in the damn safe house and being in danger.

Wolf was also scared. Being scared was a new feeling for him. He wasn't scared for himself, he never was. He knew what he could and couldn't do and he knew he could handle anything the terrorists threw at him. He was scared for Caroline. He'd never felt that way about another human being before in his life. He always could take or leave women, but not Caroline. In the short time he'd gotten to know her he was impressed as hell by her outlook on life and how she'd handled herself on that plane.

Wolf knew there weren't a lot of people that could've done what she'd done.

So he and his team, thanks to his commander back in San Diego pulling strings, were now a part of the team protecting Caroline. They had no idea who the double agent was, but at least this way they could protect Caroline while searching for the bastard.

Abe, Benny, Dude, Mozart and Cookie were currently checking out the lay of the land around the cabin the FBI had stashed her in. They were setting up perimeters and making sure that nothing could get to the cabin without first alerting them. The men would take turns being on watch. There was no question about who would be in the cabin with Caroline. That was Wolf's woman in there, and they'd all protect their team leader and his woman.

Caroline didn't know what the hell was going on, only that she'd been thinking about Matthew and suddenly he was there. He looked wonderful. Strong, capable...and completely out of her league. Caroline smiled back at Matthew absently then went back into her room and shut the door. This was going to kill her. She wasn't sure what he was doing there, but obviously the FBI agent was expecting him.

After a bit of time had passed, Wolf knocked softly on Caroline's door.

"May I come in, Ice?" he asked. When there was no answer he turned the knob and opened the door. Caroline was sitting on the bed, her back against the wall, knees up to her chest with her arms grasping them tightly. She looked heartbreakingly vulnerable.

Wolf left the door open and walked over where she was sitting. He sat down gingerly at the end of the bed. It took everything he had not to take her in his arms and hold her tight. She scared the hell out of him with her phone message and it wasn't until right now, seeing she was okay, that he could slightly relax.

"What are you doing here, Matthew?" She asked softly.

"I'm here because you're here," he answered honestly.

Caroline just shook her head. "I don't understand. You don't really know me. I don't understand why you'd be here. You can't be here."

Matthew knew she was confused. Hell, he was a bit confused himself. He tried to explain. "There's something between us, Caroline," he said honestly. "I can't explain it any better than you can. The kisses we shared were the most honest and arousing I've ever had in my life. You *know* how badly I wanted to lay you down and love you all night long. You have no idea how you tested my willpower every night when I tucked you into your bed. I wanted to join you there and show you how much I liked you, being with you."

Caroline sucked in a breath, not believing what he was saying.

"Yeah, you heard me right. I got harder just kissing you than any other time I've been with a woman. But it's not only sex. I like you. You're intelligent, fun to be around, and I want to know everything about you. When I heard you were in trouble, there was no place I needed to be more than here with you. Protecting you. Making sure you're safe." When she didn't say anything, but continued to stare at him with her big brown eyes, he asked, "Why did you really call me that day in your apartment Caroline? Be honest."

Caroline sighed. He was right. Matthew deserved the truth. She didn't know what was going on with the two of them, but whatever it was, at least he seemed to feel it too.

Her voice trembling with emotion and just above a whisper, she told him honestly, "I called you because you were the first person I thought of when I was scared. I called you because if I died, I wanted you to know I was thinking about you, that I wanted to see you again. I didn't want you to come back to Norfolk and think I didn't want to go to see you again. I wanted it more than you know, and I thought I wouldn't have a chance..." Her voice trailed off.

Wolf didn't say anything, just did what he'd desired to do the first time he saw her in the room. He reached over and gathered her into his arms. She was stiff at first, then she melted into him. She smelled of some sort of flowers. Maybe it was her shampoo, maybe it was a lotion she used, but it went straight to his head. He tightened his arms around her and Caroline lost it. She cried. She cried for being scared on the plane, she cried for being hurt, she cried remembering how alone and scared she felt in her apartment when only a thin piece of plastic kept a killer from knowing she was in the bathroom, she cried in relief that Matthew was back from his mission. Matthew rocked her and held her tight. He wasn't used to a woman's tears, but there was no way he was letting her go.

Finally her tears dried up and she only sniffed here and there. Wolf drew back a bit and looked at her face. She wasn't a "cute crier"—her face was red and blotchy. She refused to raise her eyes. Wolf rubbed her cheeks with his thumbs and then lifted her chin up so Caroline had to look at him. He didn't say anything just leaned down and touched her lips with his. It wasn't a passionate kiss, but it felt right. It was a comforting kiss. It was exactly what she needed from him at that moment.

He pulled back and looked into her eyes. "You're safe now. I'll do everything in my power to make sure you stay that way."

Caroline believed him. He was an honest-to-God hero. And for the moment, he was *her* hero. She tipped her chin up, reaching again for his lips with hers.

The second she moved, he was there. Wolf had tried to hold back with her. She was feeling vulnerable and he didn't want to take advantage of her. But with the first touch of her lips against him, he was lost.

He devoured her. He stroked her tongue with his and she stroked his right back. He fell back on the bed taking her down with him. He could feel every inch of her delectable body against his. She was curvy and soft and he could feel her nipples harden against his chest.

He wrapped his hand in her hair and moved her head where he wanted it. He took complete control of the kiss and rolled them until she was under him. Wolf felt her leg bend and it opened herself up to him even more. He settled into the vee of her legs and felt his erection burrow into the heat in Caroline's center. Christ. He had to stop. Now. Or there'd be no stopping. It was the thought of the FBI agent in the other room that finally made Wolf stop. Hell, he hadn't even shut the door behind him. When he took Caroline it wouldn't be in some crappy cabin with someone who may or may not be a traitor to their country listening nearby.

Wolf eased back, but couldn't bear to break contact with her. He buried his head into her neck and licked and suckled at her earlobe. The whimpering that came from her throat made him grow even harder. She arched into him, trying to get closer. She was sexy as hell.

"Jesus, sweetheart. I'd give anything to take this where we both want to go, but I can't, not now, not here, and not while you're in danger." He hoped like hell Caroline wouldn't be offended by his words.

Caroline shut her eyes tightly. God, Matthew felt so good against her. She was wet. She hadn't ever gotten so wet so quickly with any other man before. Just Matthew. Only him. When she felt him shift above her she slowly opened her eyes. Jesus. He was so sexy, and he was here, with her. That alone was a miracle. She saw the hard line of his jaw and his kiss-swollen lips. She wanted nothing more than to have him strip off all her clothes, but unfortunately, she knew he was right.

"I-I know. Will you stay? Here? With me?" Caroline was a little embarrassed to even ask, but she needed him. She needed his closeness; she needed the safety his embrace promised.

"Of course, sweetheart." Without letting go, he moved them up further onto the bed and turned them on their sides. Wolf tucked Caroline into his big frame. Her back was to his front and they lay there in silence for a few minutes. Wolf had one arm under her head and the other was wrapped around her tightly. His forearm rested between her breasts and his hand rested on her shoulder. She was cocooned in his arms, and it felt heavenly.

"What's going on, Matthew?" Caroline asked sleepily.

"Shhhhh. I'll tell you everything tomorrow," he told her. "Just sleep now. I've got you."

Caroline fell asleep almost immediately. She felt safe for the first time in a long time. Matthew was here, he wouldn't let anything happen to her. Even while unconscious, in the depths of sleep, her body knew she was safe. She didn't have one nightmare that night.

Chapter Fifteen

T HE NEXT FEW days went by without anything interesting happening. Matthew came by the cabin each night, but left early each morning. He'd told her, he and his team were here and they were keeping watch, but she hadn't seen anyone but Matthew. She would've liked to have talked to Christopher and Sam, but she was way out of her element. She didn't ask Matthew any questions, outside of the obvious ones. She didn't ask where his team was, she trusted him to make sure she was safe.

Matthew slept with her each night. They'd shared more of those soul searching kisses, but he hadn't let anything more happen. On one hand it was driving her crazy, but at the same time she understood he was "working"—they'd have to wait. For now, it was enough to be able to fall asleep cuddled up in his arms, safe. She wasn't convinced Matthew could *really* want someone like her, but she held out hope. He was convincing her one night at a time. She hoped the bounty on her head would be taken care of soon and then they could figure out where they stood.

Caroline thought sometimes it was all just too ridiculous. She lived in Norfolk now and Matthew lived in San Diego...when he was even in the country. She didn't begrudge him his job, but knew it was tough to be involved with any military man, but most especially a SEAL. But at this point in their relationship, Caroline could honestly say she wanted to give them a shot. Matthew was the best thing to happen to her in a long time, she didn't want to give it up yet.

It wasn't just because of the way he looked either. Caroline supposed that was a part of it, but it was more the kind of man he was. He was loyal, smart, and attentive. Matthew paid attention to her as if she was the most important thing in his life. She knew if they stayed together, she'd come first in his life—before his friends and even before the military...if at all possible. She'd be an idiot to let him go. If Matthew wanted to see where their relationship could go after all the crap with this was over, she was all for it.

Caroline wasn't sure what had woken her up, but when she went to roll over she felt Matthew's large hand cover her mouth. She stiffened. She knew it was Matthew behind her because she could smell his unique scent, but he was as still as a statue and was as tense as she'd ever felt him. She felt him lean down toward her head.

"Don't make a sound. Okay?" he whispered tonelessly, directly into her ear.

Caroline nodded and he lifted his hand from her mouth. He rolled off the bed soundlessly, a pistol materializing in his hand. Caroline didn't know where the gun came from, but was glad to see he was armed. She watched as he took the time to push his feet into a pair of boots.

She was afraid to move, but forced herself to sit up and scoot over to the edge of the bed. If she had to move quickly, she wanted to be ready. She also leaned over and slipped on her shoes sitting next to the bed. Caroline couldn't hear anything at all, but he'd obviously heard something out of the ordinary.

Wolf listened at the bedroom door. He eased the bedroom door open and still didn't hear or see anything. He looked back at Caroline sitting on the bed. The last few days had been hell, holding her, kissing her, but not making love to her. He wanted to bury himself so far inside her she'd *know* she was his, but he held back. It wasn't the time or the place, but he hoped it would be soon. They were making progress. Each day he and his team met and went over documents, and he felt they were narrowing in on the double crosser.

Wolf held his finger to his lips and motioned for Caroline to stay where she was. He saw her nod once and eased out of the room. He was very proud of her. She hadn't panicked and didn't ask any questions. She understood what was at stake and trusted him to do his job. That trust made him feel ten feet tall. He wouldn't let her down.

Wolf pushed thoughts of Caroline out of his head and concentrated on figuring out what was wrong. He had a job to do and he knew he couldn't do it if he was thinking about her. The gut feeling that something wasn't right was what had woken him up. He thought he'd heard something, but wasn't sure. He wasn't willing to let it go, not when it meant Caroline's safety.

He eased his way into the small outer room, trying to figure out what, if anything was wrong. He looked right and left, then stopped suddenly. Shit. He smelled gas. Just as he took a step back toward the bedroom door, the front of the cabin went up in flames in one big *whoosh*.

Wolf was knocked backwards by the wave of heat. He lay on the floor for just a moment getting his bearings. Before he could get up again, the wall on the other side of the cabin went up in flames. Matthew couldn't catch his breath. The flames had sucked all the oxygen out of the room in an instant. He tried to crawl back down the hall toward Caroline. He had to get to her. Where the hell was his team? He had no idea what had gone wrong, but it was obvious something bad had happened to them. There was no way anyone could've slipped by them in order to torch the cabin.

The terrorists had done their job well, and cut off both exits from the cabin, they were trapped. The last thought he had before he passed out from breathing the super-heated toxic air, was of Caroline, and disgust with himself that he'd let her down.

Caroline didn't move from her spot on the bed until she heard the first explosion. She leaped from the bed and ran for the bedroom door. What the hell? The heat coming from the main room almost drove her back. She got on her hands and knees and, without thinking twice about what she was doing, crawled into the burning room.

She saw Matthew on the floor and then the other wall burst into flames. Caroline ducked and covered her head with her hands. Shit. Shit. Shit. She'd managed not to squeal like a little girl, but a terrified croak escaped before she could call it back.

She looked up and saw Matthew try to crawl toward her and then fall down unmoving. Caroline didn't stop to think. She fast-crawled over to him, grabbed him under the arms, much like she'd done with the terrorist on the plane, and hauled him back to the bedroom. It was a slow process because Matthew was heavy and the exertion plus the smoke filling the room was making it tough to move quickly.

The cabin was quickly filling with smoke. It wasn't until she'd gotten Matthew back into the room and shut the door she realized they were trapped in the house. She ran to the attached bathroom grabbed a towel, quickly soaked it in water from the tap, and stuffed it along the bottom of the door to the bedroom. It reduced the smoke coming into the room a bit, but not all the way. The bedroom was going to fill with smoke sooner rather than later, and it wouldn't be long before the flames were burning through the entire wall.

Caroline grabbed two of her T-shirts from the drawer. She ran into the bathroom, well aware of the time that was ticking by, and soaked them with water in the sink. She put one around her nose and mouth and ran back to Matthew. He was still lying where she'd left him on the floor. She tied the other T-shirt awkwardly around his head. She had to protect him from the smoke making its way into the room. Caroline was operating completely on auto-pilot now.

She ran to the only window in the room. She cautiously drew back the curtain and looked out.

BAM

Caroline leaped back and crouched down just as the window shattered. She couldn't help but scream out in fright this time and she covered her head as the glass from the window rained down on her. Crap. She crawled over to where Matthew lay on the ground motionless.

"This would be a really good time to wake up Matthew," she said shakily as she pried the pistol out of his hand. She shook him once, hard. He didn't respond and Caroline allowed one desperate sob to escape before she beat it back. If she started crying now, she wouldn't be able to stop.

It looked like the terrorists had found her. They'd set the front and side of the cabin on fire to force her into this room, and the only escape was the window…only there were obviously men out there waiting for her to leave that way. She was going to die. She didn't want to die and she definitely didn't want Matthew to die either. She wasn't going to give up until it was too late. She wasn't a SEAL, but was there anything she could do?

She tried to think like a soldier, what would Matthew do if he was conscious? As she eased her way back to the window and couldn't see any bad guys she deflated a bit. How was she supposed to defend herself with the gun she now held in her hand, if she couldn't even see who she was supposed to shoot?

Caroline allowed a few stray tears to leak out of her eyes. What was the best way to die? Burning to death? Smoke inhalation? Getting shot? Shit. None of the choices were good ones. She had to get herself together. Matthew wouldn't just give up. If it was her lying unconscious on the ground he'd do whatever he had to do to keep her safe. She'd do the same.

She tried to think. Caroline had to believe Matthew's team would get to her. He'd said they were patrolling around the cabin. They'd get here soon; she'd act as if they were out there right now figuring out how to get both her and Matthew out. She risked a glance out the window again. There! She finally saw someone, a man off to the right. She stuck the pistol out the window and pulled the trigger. The kickback of the gun was more than she was ready for and she fell backward with the force of it. She heard yelling outside, then silence again. Had she hit him? She doubted it. She risked another glance. Nope, they were still there.

The smoke in the room was getting thicker. She went back to Matthew and hauled him closer to the window, trying to avoid the glass on the ground. She wasn't sure how they were going to get out of this, but she wasn't leaving Matthew behind. Wasn't there some SEAL code on that? She tried to think back. Yeah, Christopher had said something about it to her in the airport when they'd come to find her.

Well, she wasn't a SEAL, but she wasn't leaving Matthew behind to die in this stupid cabin. The only reason he was there was because of *her*. She wouldn't be able to live with herself if he was killed because of her. Shit. She had to stop thinking about Matthew being dead.

Just as she was gearing up to look out the window again she heard more shots. She hoped it was a good sign. She reasoned that since there were no bullets coming through the walls of her prison, it had to be. Hopefully it was the Calvary coming to their rescue. After a short period of time she heard a voice calling urgently from outside.

"Wolf? Ice?"

Caroline risked peeking out the window again. It was Sam. He was standing outside the window. She stood up and blurted, "Here!"

Mozart was never as glad to see anyone as he was to see Ice. When the cabin had gone up in flames he'd been surprised. Someone, or some people, had obviously made their way past their recon around the perimeter of the cabin. He'd immediately set out to find the culprits and get Wolf and his woman out of the cabin.

"Where's Wolf?" he demanded urgently.

"He's here, but he's unconscious." Caroline stopped to cough. She had no idea trying to breathe when in a burning building would hurt so much. Again, stupid, but how was she supposed to know?

"Let's get you out, then we'll get him." Mozart ordered. He'd holstered his pistol and reached up for her. The window was on the first floor, but since the land sloped down on this side of the cabin, it was about a five foot drop to the ground. Caroline shook her head.

"No. Matthew first."

Mozart started to disagree, but Caroline disappeared from the window. Damn. He didn't have time to argue with her. He wasn't sure if there were any other terrorists around, but he knew Ice and Wolf were running out of time. The roof was on fire and the entire cabin was about to go up in flames. He saw Ice struggling with Wolf's inert body near the window. He grabbed the window sill to pull himself in and help, but let go quickly. The metal around the window was red hot.

"Careful, Ice," Mozart said urgently. "It's really hot."

Caroline nodded. She heard him, but didn't take her eyes off Matthew. He'd groaned a few times, she hoped he was coming out of it. She quickly dragged him as close as she could to the window and untied the T-shirt from around her face and laid it over the window sill. She heard it sizzling as the wet cloth met the red hot metal of the sill. She pushed as hard as she could until Matthew was lying on his stomach right under the window.

Caroline grabbed Matthew again and hauled him up as close as she could get him to the open window. She draped his arms outside and yelled at Sam to grab him. With Sam's help, she pushed, and Mozart pulled, and Matthew slid out of the house. Caroline quickly looked out and saw that Sam had mostly caught him and was easing him to the ground taking the T-shirt off his face as he laid him on the ground.

"Okay, come on, Ice. I've got you." Mozart held up his arms to help her get out of the burning cabin.

Caroline shook her head again, "No, take Matthew and go, I'm right behind you. I don't need help. Just get him out of here and safe."

Mozart was frustrated, but she was right. He had to get Wolf out of there. He leaned down and put his teammate over his shoulder in a fireman's carry.

"Okay, I've got him; get your ass out of there. *Now!*" Mozart bellowed at Ice.

Caroline ignored the ire in Sam's voice. She knew he was stressed and wasn't really yelling at her. She turned around to look around the room to see what she could use to help her get out of the window and not get burned. The T-shirt she'd laid there to protect Matthew had slid out with his body.

She grabbed a pillow off the bed. She laid it over the hot window sill and watched as it too immediately started to smoke. It was now or never. She didn't have any time to spare. She stuck one leg, then the other out the window and sat on the pillow on the sill. She took one more look behind her and saw the bedroom wall collapsing. She let out a small shriek and jumped. It wasn't too far to the ground but she fell sideways when she landed anyway. She immediately got up and headed after Sam.

Mozart took the time to turn and look at Ice as they ran away from the burning cabin. She was next to him. She had cuts on her arms and legs from the glass from the window, her face was covered in soot, she was coughing like a forty year old smoker, but she was mobile and running. It had to be good enough for now.

"Why didn't you get out of there, Ice?" Mozart asked, not even out of breath. He was obviously in good shape and this was just another little run for him.

"SEALs don't leave SEALs," Caroline panted and said between coughs. "I couldn't leave him. I just couldn't."

Just as they were reaching the nearby tree line, a man stepped out from behind a tree, holding a pistol pointed right at them.

"Stop right there," he said menacingly.

Mozart knew he could take him. No problem. As he was leaning over to set Wolf on the ground he saw more men come out of the trees, all with rifles or pistols pointed at them. Shit. He was good, but he wasn't *that* good. Where was the team?

"I bet you're wondering where your team is, aren't you?" The man sneered, seemingly reading his mind. "They aren't coming. They've been 'indisposed,'" he threw his head back and laughed in the most evil laugh

Caroline had ever heard.

"You've been a pain in my butt for a while now bitch, but now it's my turn to be one step ahead. You SEALs think you're indestructible, but you aren't."

Before any of them could do anything, the man raised his pistol and shot at Mozart. Mozart felt the bullet graze his head and he fell sharply to the ground. Hell, that hurt. He heard Ice screaming. God, Ice. He felt Wolf's bodyweight heavy on his back. He tried not to pass out. He needed to stay awake and get Caroline out of there. He needed to protect her and make sure Wolf was all right.

Caroline screamed as she watched Sam fall to the ground still holding Matthew. Two men came out from the trees toward her and grabbed her before she could even think about running or fighting back. She struggled and tried to kick them, but they had her arms bound behind her back before she could do anything.

The zip ties they'd used immediately bit into her flesh. They'd tightened them to the point of cutting off her circulation. They obviously weren't concerned about her comfort. That scared her more than anything.

"No, stop it. What are you doing?" She said, still struggling in the grip of the two men and against her bindings. They walked her toward the man that had shot Sam.

"You're coming with us, bitch," the man smirked

and backhanded her hard across the face. Caroline would've fallen to the ground if she wasn't being held up by the other two men. Dammit, that hurt. Her head swam. She coughed. Jesus, she was in trouble here.

Mozart struggled on the ground. He'd heard what the man had said. Shit, he had to get to Ice; he couldn't let this guy take her. His head was swimming and he couldn't get his arms to work right. He was going to pass out; he wasn't going to be able to help her.

The man turned his attention back to Sam and Matthew on the ground. He held the pistol toward them.

"No. No. *No!*" Caroline screamed, struggling even harder, ignoring the pain in her arms from the awkward way she was being held. "Leave them alone. What do you want? Me? You've got me, leave them alone!"

The man turned back toward Carline with a glint in his eye. "You don't want me to kill them?" He said with venom.

Caroline shook her head vigorously.

The man laughed evilly. "What will you do for me if I let them live?"

Caroline was scared out of her mind. She had no idea what this man had in store for her, but she knew he wasn't really asking for her permission. He'd kill them in a heartbeat if he wanted to. "Whatever you want. I'll do whatever you want. Just don't kill them. They're only here because of me." She'd drop to her knees if she thought it would help, but the man didn't even give her a chance to offer.

The man turned his back on her and went over to Sam and Matthew. He pulled a knife out of his pocket and leaned down toward Sam. Before Caroline could beg the man not to hurt him he'd sliced into Sam's cheek. Laughing he did it again, and again. Standing upright again he brought his boot down and ground it in Sam's face as if he was squishing a bug under his foot.

Turning toward Caroline, who was now watching in horror, he sneered, "Fine, I won't kill them, but they'll wish they were dead when my men get through with them. They've got other ways to make them suffer." He nodded at two other men nearby and they headed for Sam and Matthew.

Caroline struggled with all her might but all it did was make her wrists bleed sluggishly. The last thing she saw as she was led away was the two men kicking Sam and Matthew who lay unconscious on the ground.

Chapter Sixteen

WOLF PACED THE room. It'd been six hours since Caroline had been taken. His throat was still raw from smoke inhalation, and he was still coughing, but he was alive. He was glad he didn't remember the beating he and Mozart had been given on the field. The rest of the team had arrived in time to prevent the two thugs from killing them.

The terrorists were good. They'd created a diversion that had Benny, Dude, and Cookie headed off on a wild-goose-chase. Wolf only knew what his team had told him they'd seen when they came across the terrorists beating the crap out of him and Mozart, which wasn't much. He had no idea what had happened to Caroline and how they'd gotten out of the cabin. Mozart had most likely rescued the both of them and they'd been overwhelmed while escaping.

Mozart was still unconscious. A bullet had grazed his head and that, along with the beating, had him laid up in the hospital. Wolf was especially worried about

Mozart's face as well. Someone had carved him up and there was enough dirt and crap in his wounds to cause a massive infection. Mozart had always been the "pretty" one of their crew and Wolf worried that his days of being a flirt would be over. His face wasn't pretty, but at this point that wasn't what was concerning the doctors. They'd all just have to wait and to see how long it'd take him to pull out of it. Dude, Abe, Benny, Cookie and himself were now trying to figure out what the hell happened and where the fuck Caroline was.

Wolf hurt, but he ignored his injuries. He'd suffered worse in the past and continued on. This time was different though, they had his Caroline. He closed his eyes in despair, then quickly opened them again. He didn't have time to feel sorry for himself or to panic. He had to figure out what the hell was going on and where Caroline was. It was time to call Tex. If anyone could find her, it was Tex.

CAROLINE OPENED HER eyes slowly. She hurt. Everywhere. She had no idea where she was. The man who'd kidnapped her had stuffed her into an SUV and one of the other men had knocked her out with a cloth over her nose and mouth. She knew it was chloroform, and fought as hard as she could, but inevitably, couldn't fight its effects.

When she'd come to, she was restrained to this stupid chair. The damn zip ties were still on her wrists, but now they were attached to the arms of the chair she was sitting in. She could see the blood oozing over the edge of the armrests and dripping onto the floor. Jesus, it was like a bad movie. The chair, the zip ties, the chloroform...if it hadn't been happening to her and if she wasn't so scared, it would've been laughable.

The man who'd cut Sam and ordered both him and Matthew beaten—she hoped they weren't killed, despite what he'd said—came into the room. She was in some sort of warehouse. He came right up to her and spit in her face. Caroline was so surprised she didn't do anything to try to avoid the spittle. She felt it ooze down her cheek as he yelled at her.

"You stupid bitch," the man growled at her. "You cost me *everything*! I had it all planned. It was gonna work, and you blew it. *You*. It's all *your* fault! Those dumb ass country hick SEALs wouldn't have known what was going on if it wasn't for you."

The man continued his ranting. "You'll tell me everything that happened on that plane. I want to know exactly how you knew about the ice and how you overpowered my men!"

Caroline didn't want to tell him anything. It was enough he knew she was involved. She'd never been so scared in all her life. Even when she was hiding in the shower afraid to breathe too loud, she hadn't been *this* frightened. Jesus, each situation she'd been in was worse than the last. This time she knew she was going to die. The government didn't make deals with terrorists and besides that, no one even knew where she was. Matthew and Sam had been unconscious when she'd been dragged out of the clearing by the cabin, and she hadn't seen anyone else around. If his men *had* been around, they would've prevented them from taking her...wouldn't they?

Even as the brief thought flashed through her head that maybe they let the terrorists take her to save their teammates, she dismissed it. She hadn't met the rest of the team yet, but if they were anything like Matthew, hell, like Christopher or Sam, they wouldn't have let them take her. She had to get control of herself. Thinking irrationally wasn't going to save her life. If she had any chance of getting out of this clusterfuck, she had to use her brain.

Even though she was scared, she vowed to herself she wasn't going to tell this maniac anything that would help him take down another plane or hurt more people. She looked away from the man and around the room instead. To even have a chance, she had to start trying to figure out how to get out of there.

"You aren't going to talk, bitch?"

Caroline's eyes went back to the crazy man standing

in front of her. She just looked at him without saying a word.

He leaned in toward her. Caroline could smell the foul body odor coming off of him. It was as if he hadn't showered in days, no weeks. He leaned in as a lover would, and whispered into her ear.

"You tell me what happened or I'll make you so miserable you'll be begging me to let you tell me every little thing I want to know. Then you'll beg me to kill you." He licked the side of her neck up to her ear with a long slow brush of his tongue against her. Then he bit her earlobe so hard Caroline was afraid he'd torn it in two. She couldn't help but whimper and try to pull away from the pain. She didn't want to tell him anything, but she wasn't tough. She was just…her.

The man stood up and backhanded her. He didn't give her a chance to recover from his strike before hitting her again, then again. Then he kicked her shin as hard as he could. He continued hitting her and slapping her and occasionally biting her. He tried everything he could to get her to talk, but Caroline kept her mouth shut.

Caroline started off stoic and not giving any reaction to each strike, but she was soon crying out with every hit and she could feel the tears coursing down her cheeks. The man knew he was hurting her, but he didn't stop. He laughed as he beat her.

Caroline knew she was going to die, but she'd be dammed before this crazy man used her knowledge to hurt or kill others. She said nothing throughout his beating, just kept trying to avoid his fists and feet when she could, which wasn't often.

Finally he stopped. Caroline knew it wasn't because of anything she'd done, but more because he was tired. He was breathing hard, and panting as if he'd run a couple of miles. He was sweating profusely and his face was bright red.

"You're a stupid bitch. Don't worry, I'm leaving you for now, but I'll be back. We'll start up where I left off. I'll bring some of my buddies back with me. You can just sit there and think about all the ways I can make you hurt before I kill you, slowly. I'll give my men a go at you as well. Have you ever been gang banged? No? Well you just sit there and think about it. You can save yourself the pain and misery if you'd just tell me what I want to know. If you do, I'll kill you quickly. If not, you'll die a horribly painful death. I can promise you that. My men will make sure you're bleeding out of every hole before they kill you. They'll watch you bleed and laugh." He spit on her once more and left the room.

Caroline's head bobbed. She closed her eyes and tried to process everything. She was still tied up in the chair and had blood dripping from her head somewhere. Her eyes were almost swollen shut. But she was still alive...for now. She completely believed the man when he said he'd make her suffer. She'd seen the look the men who'd roughly pushed her into the SUV had given her. They wouldn't be gentle at all with her. She was scared shitless. She didn't want to die slowly, or otherwise, but she just couldn't, and wouldn't, condemn other innocent people to die.

Caroline tried to figure out more about where she was. If she had a shot at all to get out of there she had to pay attention. She couldn't see that well through her swollen eyes and the blood blurring her vision, so she tried to listen.

There...what was that? Seagulls. The nasty birds always made those cawing sounds as they flew through the air. She had to be by the sea. She felt proud of herself for a moment, but then realized most of Norfolk was by the ocean. Crap. That wasn't going to help anyone. She could hear what sounded like ship horns blowing. She tried to concentrate more, but finally just closed her eyes. She was so tired...

It could have been minutes or hours later when she heard the door squeak open in the cavernous room. A man came in, not the same man that had beaten her before. She'd never seen him before, but he was wearing a three piece black suit. His hair was slicked back and not a piece was askew. He looked as out of place in the dungeon-like atmosphere of the filthy room as he would've at a rodeo in the heart of Texas. He was followed by three other men, including the guy who'd beaten her earlier. *Oh shit. Was this it?* Caroline held in a sob. She regretted with every fiber of her being not making love with Matthew. She suddenly fervently wished she'd put her concerns about moving too fast with him aside and had gone for it.

The man in the suit didn't look at her, didn't say anything. He got busy setting up what looked like a tripod. Oh God. Was he going to *film* the men raping her? He mounted the video camera on the tripod and turned it around so it was facing her. He stood behind it and gave a chin lift to the three other men. Caroline saw the red light blinking on the camera and shuddered, watching as the men came toward her, cracking their knuckles. No, no, no, she couldn't do this. She screeched as they reached for her.

WOLF SAT AT the table, his hands clenched in his lap. He was a SEAL. He was supposed to be able to save the world, but he felt helpless because he couldn't save the one person who'd quickly come to mean everything to him. He and his team had discussed for what seemed like hours what they were going to do next. Tex was working frantically with his hacker friends to try and track down where the men had taken Caroline. They had some clues, but no location, not yet. Cookie's phone rang and he answered it quickly.

"Yes, sir. Got it. I'll tell him." He hung up. "Check your email, Wolf." Cookie said. "That was the commander, he just received a video. He told me to tell you they were tracing it now."

Cookie called Tex to update him on the email and to have him get to work tracing it. They knew the commander was tracing it as well, but more often than not Tex could get results faster than anyone else. Wolf quickly brought up his email on the laptop and the team gathered around to watch.

The five men watched in horror and anger. It wasn't anything they hadn't seen or experienced for themselves in the past. But this was Caroline. Wolf's Ice. That made all the difference in the world.

The video showed Caroline strapped to a chair. She'd obviously been beaten. Her wrists were bleeding where the zip ties held her to the chair and she had blood dripping from her head somewhere. But her face. Jesus. They'd beaten the hell out of her. Her eyes were swollen almost shut, and her face was already bruising. The T-shirt she was wearing was ripped and hanging off of one shoulder. They could see her bra strap vividly white against her skin. She was breathing quickly and erratically.

There was a man speaking, but Wolf barely heard

him. *His* woman was hurt. Christ. He couldn't handle this. He pushed pause on the video and locked his hands behind his head. He paced back and forth rapidly. He took a deep breath. He *had* to handle it. He couldn't let Caroline down. He had to focus.

His teammates let him be. No one tried to talk to him. No one gave him false reassurances. They didn't know what they were going to see on the rest of the tape. It was up to Wolf on when, and if, he wanted to watch the rest of the video.

Wolf paced, trying to gather up the courage to watch the rest of the video. If his woman was killed in front of his eyes, he didn't know how he'd react. He had to lock it down. Wanting to go back to the previous night when he'd held Caroline's soft sweet body in his arms, Wolf took a deep breath. "*Fuck.*" All his anguish and dread were put into that one word. The room was quiet. No one said anything; they could feel Wolf's anguish.

He finally spun toward the laptop and clicked the mouse that would start the awful video again.

"Tell me what happened!" The man beating her screamed. At her silence he continued screeching at her. "How did you know the ice was drugged? I *know* it was you. Those dumb ass SEALs don't have the smarts to know their head from their ass. I know it wasn't them. What tipped you off? How did they get the jump on my men?"

The SEALs could see the man getting more and more agitated as he continued to ask Caroline questions and she refused to answer. At one point Wolf heard Cookie say under his breath, "Jesus, just tell him sweetheart. God, just tell him what he wants to know."

She didn't.

Abe paced behind the men. He couldn't watch anymore. Those bastards. How could they do that to a woman? To their Ice? Why didn't she just tell him and save herself some agony?

They watched as the man yelling at Caroline stopped asking her what she'd done and looked up toward the camera. Then he lost it, ranting at the SEALs, at how they all thought they were God's gift to the world and thought they were invincible.

The man continued to berate and hit at Caroline, but they heard a disembodied voice come from behind the camera. They hadn't realized someone else was in the room. They could only see the three men taking turns beating Caroline. "How does it feel watching my interrogation? I'm finding it quite...entertaining." The chuckle that followed the flat statement was horrifying. It suddenly became clear.

"That's the traitor," Benny said, hate clear in his tone. "That's the bastard that's behind everything."

Before anyone else could say anything, the camera

was jostled and the team realized the mysterious traitor was now holding the camera.

The SEALs all watched as the unknown man carried the camera close to Caroline. He zoomed in on her face, speaking directly to the SEALs the entire time.

"How does it feel to watch them beat her? How does it feel to see the blood falling from her skull, knowing I ordered it?" He zoomed in on her wrists. "Look at how she's struggled trying to get away from me. The zip ties are cutting off her circulation. See how her fingers are turning blue?"

He laughed then—an evil nasty laugh that sliced through Wolf and his team.

The man stood back so they had a wide angle view of Caroline in the chair. They all saw the other men come up on either side of her.

"Jesus no," Wolf moaned. He couldn't take this anymore. He turned away from the computer screen. They were going to kill her and he couldn't watch. He wouldn't stop the video again, but he'd be damned if he watched his love die. Then, changing his mind he abruptly turned back to the screen. No, he wanted to watch. He needed the motivation to keep him going after she was gone. He needed a reason to find every one of the men, and every one of the terrorists in their organization and make them pay.

The team watched as one of the men struck out and

knocked her over, still tied to the chair. She fell hard on her side. All the men could hear her grunt as her head bounced off the hard floor as she landed.

The man in charge just laughed in the background.

"That was awesome. I'm surprised her head didn't split open." The camera came close to Caroline's face again. The disembodied voice sounded again. "You want to tell me what I want to know yet, babe?" he taunted her.

"I'll tell you," Caroline mumbled while bloody saliva dripped from her battered and torn lips.

Abe moaned, actually moaned. "No, Jesus, don't." None of them knew if it was better if she kept her mouth shut or if she told this demented man what he thought he needed to know. Who knew what he'd do after she told him how she knew the ice was drugged.

Wolf leaned toward the screen as if he could will the man behind the camera to make a mistake, to step in front of the video camera just once. All he needed was one split second. Tex would do his magic and have a photo to them in no time if that happened. He saw Caroline spit some blood out of her mouth and try to lift her head off the ground. She still lay on her side, suspended in the chair she was tied to.

She sounded horrible. Her words were slurred and she mumbled her words. "You want to know what happened, asshole?"

At the man's affirmative grunt, she continued, "Well fuck you. You and your army of *gull*ible terrorists can get back on whatever party boat you sailed here on and go to hell!" She'd looked right at the camera while saying it, not at the man standing next to her, not into the eyes of the man holding the camera. It was as if she looked right into the eyes of each of the SEAL team members as she'd spoken. There was silence in the room for a moment, then the man behind the camera nonchalantly commented, "Tsk. Tsk. Tsk. Your bitch isn't very bright is she, Wolf? We'll be in touch." And the video went dark.

Wolf tried to hold it together. He was losing it. They had nothing. Nothing. He growled and kicked at a stool. It went flying across the room.

In the silence of the room Abe unexpectedly urged, "Play that last part again."

Wolf turned to him incredulously. "You want to watch that shit again? What the *fuck,* Abe?"

Abe wasn't listening. He reached over Wolf, ignoring his incredulous question and grabbed the mouse, not waiting for him to do what he'd asked. They watched Caroline being kicked and watched her stare eerily at the camera again and heard her recorded voice say, *"Well fuck you. You and your army of gullible terrorists can get back on whatever party boat you sailed here on and go to hell!"*

Abe played it again. Then again. Wolf was about to beat the hell out of his teammate. He couldn't watch it one more time without losing his shit. He couldn't hear her slurred words full of pain. He felt like his heart was breaking.

Abe turned to his teammates. "Did you catch that?"

"Hell yeah," Dude said urgently. "It's not a lot to go on, but it's a start."

Wolf shook his head and stared at his teammates. What was he missing? What had Dude and Abe caught that he'd missed? As much as he didn't want to see Caroline's battered and bruised face or hear her tortured voice one more time, he had to hear it for himself.

"Well fuck you. You and your army of gullible terrorists can get back on whatever party boat you sailed here on and go to hell!"

Suddenly he got it. Caroline was giving them clues. Gulls and party boats….she had to be somewhere near the ocean. She'd looked right at them and willed them to understand. It wasn't a lot to go on, as Norfolk was an ocean port, but the party boat remark had to mean *something*. Caroline knew the difference between the Navy ships, the container ships, and pleasure boats. They'd even had a conversation when they'd toured the base about the difference between a ship and a boat. She'd teased him about not wanting his manly SEAL ship to be called a boat. Her wording to them couldn't have been coincidence.

The men all got up from the table. Cookie was already on the phone with their commander, and Abe was on the phone with Tex. They'd find her, they had to.

Wolf thought of his woman. He loved her. Caroline was his everything. She was amazing and if he lost her he didn't know what he'd do. She could be dead right now, they could've killed her after they shut off the video, but he didn't think so.

Wolf thought again about how the guy behind the camera called him by his name. He knew him, or at least knew *of* him. They had to figure out who he was and fast. Right now Caroline was his main concern, but Wolf knew they had to stop the leak as a matter of National Security. The man would want to keep Caroline alive to taunt him. Wolf didn't know how he knew that, but if they hadn't killed her on the video, she was still alive. They were going to use her somehow; they just had to get to her before that happened.

"Hang on, Ice. We're coming for you." Wolf hoped his fervent words somehow made it through the cosmos into her heart.

Chapter Seventeen

C AROLINE DIDN'T OPEN her eyes when she heard the men return to the room. They hadn't bothered putting her upright after turning off the video camera earlier, so all she could do was lie on the floor and concentrate on breathing.

She didn't think she could take much more of the attacks. She was having trouble breathing; she thought she most likely had a broken or cracked rib or two from the last beating she'd received. She wondered if Matthew and the others had gotten her message. She didn't think it was all that clever or helpful, but maybe they could figure it out.

While she'd been waiting for the men to come back and start beating on her again, she'd realized the sounds she was hearing outside weren't sounds like she heard on the Naval docks when Matthew had taken her there. She also didn't hear anything like she'd seen at the shipping yard. So she could only conclude she was at some smaller dock. That's why she'd made she'd said 'boat' and not 'ship.' She knew Matthew would understand, she'd joked with him about living on a boat and he'd made sure to correct her. He'd been on a ship, not a boat. It was a long shot, but she had to try to give them something.

She couldn't think straight anymore. They hadn't given her anything to eat or drink. Her mouth was beyond dry and she'd kill for a drink of water. She supposed it was too much bother to feed people you were going to kill. She figured if Matthew and his team didn't find her *really* soon, it wasn't going to matter anyway.

She felt two men pick up the chair she was strapped to and set it upright again. Caroline sagged against the ropes binding her to the chair. Ouch. She felt the ropes being loosened and she almost fell back onto the floor. Her wrists were still zip-tied to the armrests so she wasn't going anywhere. She didn't try to move, she couldn't anymore. She was all out of fight. She pried her swollen eyes apart and looked at the man crouched in front of her. It was the dirty smelly one that had first threatened her with rape. The polished man in the three piece suit wasn't anywhere she could see.

"Not so arrogant now are you, bitch?" he spat, then continued as if they were having a real conversation. "It really is a pity you know. My men really wanted to take their turn with you, but they aren't interested anymore.

They wanted to see if you were as much of a spitfire while being taken from behind as you would be when they raped you on your back."

Caroline didn't even flinch. Nothing this man could say to her would faze her anymore. She knew he probably wasn't kidding, but all she cared about was how he was going to kill her. She knew it'd be unpleasant and she was trying to brace herself for any possibility. She tuned him out thinking about whether having her throat slashed open would hurt.

The man continued to talk while one of his men shoved a pair of scissors under one zip tie on her wrist to cut it off. Caroline gasped at the pain that tore through her, but she refused to cry out. She knew they were being extra brutal with her just to see if they could get her to beg them. She tried to pay attention to the smelly man as the other zip tie was cut off cruelly.

"It's too bad you wouldn't cooperate with us. We'll still succeed without you. I'll figure out what tipped you off. I'm done with this. He's done with you. I'll be sure to tell your boyfriend how pathetic you were. We're going to go for a little boat ride...I'll give you one more chance..."

When she looked away from him, refusing to consider telling him anything, he grunted and stood up. He motioned to one of his men and he came forward, leaned down and hauled her over his shoulder. Caroline screamed out in pain. Agony shot through her body. The ribs she'd *thought* might be broken, she now knew were. The pain shooting up from her ribs was almost unbearable. She gasped, it was the worst pain she'd ever felt in her entire life. She wished she could pass out.

She'd watched television in the past and felt sorry for women who'd been beaten by their boyfriends or husbands, but she'd never really thought about the pain they went through. She'd seen their black eyes and heard them say how much it hurt, but until you experienced it first-hand there was no way to describe the feeling.

Caroline wished with all her heart Matthew was here. She knew it was irrational and impossible, but she wanted him. She'd never been the type of person to rely on a man, but God, she'd do anything for him to hold her and tell her everything would be all right. He'd know what to do.

She would've cried if she had it in her, but all she could do was try to hold on to the man who was carrying her and try to breathe shallow careful breaths. With her luck he'd drop her just to laugh at her reaction. She shut her eyes. God, would this ever end?

WOLF WATCHED THE warehouse closely. They'd lucked out. Tex had sent out word to be on the lookout for suspicious activity to his vast network of military members, private investigators, cops, and hackers. After only half an hour, one of his contacts had mentioned there'd been some activity at a warehouse near where his boat was docked in the old section of Norfolk. There was a large marina nearby that had boats that cost up to a million dollars right alongside small fishing vessels.

Tex had taken that lead and followed up with it himself, finding cell phone pings and other electronic activity coming from the area. He'd hacked into a security camera on the dock and had confirmed that at least one of the men that had been beating Caroline on the video was in the area.

Wolf's team headed out there immediately, set up a perimeter, and watched for a while. They saw two of the men from the video enter the building. This was it. Wolf wanted to race in and snatch Caroline away from the lunatics, but he knew he couldn't. He had to let this play out. He'd actually put Abe in charge of the mission because he knew there was no way he could be objective. This was Caroline, *his* Ice, they were going to rescue.

The team had been on many rescue missions together in the past, and they'd most likely go on many more in the future, but they all understood at a gut level it was different this time. They were essentially rescuing one of their own. Ice belonged to Wolf; they all knew it and they all were one hundred percent devoted to getting her back alive. Not one of them was unaffected by watching her bravery on the tape.

They'd been trained how to deal with interrogation tactics and how to mitigate the effects of a beating. Hell, their time in basic training and BUD/S was more torture than most people would ever have to face. They'd had years of experience. Caroline had none, yet she'd taken what they'd done to her better than any civilian. She was as innocent as anyone else they'd ever met. She was theirs. She was Ice.

Abe had no problems with being in charge. Wolf knew that he, out of all the rest of his team, knew how much Caroline meant to him and how badly he wanted to get her back safely as well. Abe had seen her bravery in person. While Cookie, Dude, and Benny appreciated her bravery from watching the video and from what they'd heard from the others, they didn't *know* her yet. While it wasn't "just" a job to them, it was more personal for him and Abe.

They knew they couldn't just rush in. They had to wait and get the traitor behind the camera. That was the only way this would end and Caroline could be free to live her life. Wolf didn't want to think of Caroline walking away from him, but he wanted her to be able to live free of fear. This whole incident might make her think twice about having anything to do with him. If he thought it was in her best interest, he'd even push her away. But he wanted her to live. He *needed* her to live.

He hadn't thought much past getting back from his mission and seeing Caroline again, but everything that had happened in the short time they'd been back in the States had changed his outlook, especially now that he'd held her in his arms for a few nights. He didn't want to let her go. He wouldn't let her go if she showed even half the interest in him that he had for her.

As the group watched the warehouse, two men exited with Caroline thrown over one of their shoulders. Wolf watched as she tried to prop herself up with her arms on the guy's back, but she was having trouble. It took Abe's hand on his arm for him to realize he'd been about to rush the men right then and there. It went against every protective bone in his body to allow the men to carry her further and further away from him and not do anything about it. He *knew* they had to find the man behind the attempted hijacking of the plane, but knowing almost wasn't enough. They watched as the trio headed toward the boats lined up on the dock on the other side.

Wolf and Abe moved around the building silently. Wolf trusted Benny was still in position. On a hunch, they'd set him up undercover. Hopefully the scumbags wouldn't recognize him from the cabin. No one knew if the terrorists had actually seen the other members of the team or not, but they had to take the chance. Wolf figured even if they did see Benny, they wouldn't recognize him the way he was disguised.

Bennie'd dressed as a fisherman who was cleaning his fish near the dock. They wanted to get as much information as they could before they moved in. If the terrorists tried to move Caroline, they wanted Benny there to listen and see what he could find out. If they did transport her by water, they needed to know which boat she was on. There were too many boats for them to have to guess where she was. They all knew they wouldn't get another chance to find her. This was it.

They watched as the terrorists drew near to where Benny was.

"She had too much to drink, huh?" Benny laughed, acting as if he'd had one too many beers that day while fishing.

The man carrying Caroline made sure to keep her head away from Benny. He smacked her ass and said, "Yeah, something like that." They didn't stick around to chat, but kept walking, keeping their eye on Benny.

Benny stood up as they passed him. He made no move to interfere with their movements, knowing he was out numbered, and essentially on a recon mission. After they passed he sat back down and pretended to go back to work on his fish again.

Seeing the fisherman do nothing suspicious, the men turned around and walked briskly toward the dock.

Caroline lifted her head to try to get the drunken fisherman to notice her. She had to make someone see that this wasn't normal, that she was hurt; she had to get some message out. When she lifted her head, she saw the fisherman staring back at her. She didn't want anyone else drawn into this, but she had to do something. She opened her mouth to say something; she didn't know what, but something. But before she could get anything out, they started around a corner of the dock.

Just before they went around a small building she thought she saw the fisherman raise his hand. It looked like he was trying to tell her something, but it was too late. They'd turned the corner and he was out of sight. Caroline was too tired to cry. She'd blown her last chance, she knew it. Her head drooped. She didn't know how much more she could take.

Benny watched as the group disappeared around the corner. Shit. He'd tried to let Ice know they were there, they were coming for her, but he'd waited too long and he didn't know if she knew what he'd been trying to tell her. He'd signaled the sign for "help is coming," but didn't see any recognition in her eyes and no acknowledgement of his signal.

Benny gathered up the fish and the basket he'd been pretending to clean and walked seemingly nonchalantly toward the warehouse. He had to meet up with his team and get their speedboat ready. He'd seen the boat they were taking her to. One part of him was glad the rescue was moving to the water. SEALs were generally always prepared for any kind of fight, but there was nothing better than bringing a battle to the water. It was what they were trained for.

CAROLINE BARELY WINCED as she was thrown onto a seat on a small motor boat. She was beyond pain at this point. Oh she still hurt, but her upcoming death was overcoming her feelings of pain.

The men didn't spare her a glance as they readied the boat to leave. She thought about jumping overboard, but didn't think that would help her much. She knew she was a good swimmer, but they'd just fish her right back out. Besides, she wasn't sure how well she'd fare in the water with her injuries. With her luck, the blood still oozing from her wrists and head would attract a shark and she'd get eaten.

The men were planning on continuing to torture her, she had no doubt. They didn't want her to die a nice, painless death. She decided she'd be better off biding her time and waiting to see what they had planned. If she had the opportunity, maybe she could slip overboard when they weren't looking. Once they got out to sea she had a better chance. It was getting dark and the lack of light would help her. She just had to wait and try to be patient.

She watched the men bumble around the boat getting it ready to push off from the dock. Just as they were about to leave, the smelly man and the man in the suit joined them. The smelly man walked right over to her and smacked her hard across the face, then laughed. The fancy man, as she dubbed him, ignored her and went into the small pilot room. She was dead. She knew it.

WOLF WAS GLAD the sun was going down. It'd work in their favor. His skin was crawling. He was ready to have Caroline back in his arms and out of danger. They followed the motor boat from a distance. It wasn't as if they'd lose them on the open ocean. It made it trickier to follow them without their knowledge, but after a while it wouldn't make a difference if the terrorists knew they were there or not. It'd just be a matter of catching up to them before they could kill Caroline.

Wolf knew their boat was more powerful than the one the terrorists were in, but again, he wanted to wait and see what they were going to do. In any rescue, the goal was to get the captured person back alive. Until they knew what the terrorists had up their sleeve, they couldn't guarantee Caroline's safety.

Wolf and his men watched from a distance as the

traitor boarded the boat. They weren't close enough to see him clearly though. Wolf sat silent and still, almost too still. Every fiber of his being was focused on the boat slicing through the choppy water ahead of them. All of the men who'd hit his woman were on that boat. If he had his way, they'd all die today; after he got Caroline safely away.

CAROLINE HUNG ON to the side of the seat, wincing every time the boat hit a wave. Her ribs hurt like hell. She tried to ignore it and concentrate on where they were. If she had to swim back to shore, she wanted to be sure she was going the right way. It would be just her luck to escape from terrorists only to swim *out* to sea instead of toward shore.

After navigating what seemed like miles, the boat finally stopped. The man in the suit came out of the wheelhouse and watched silently as one of the other men grabbed her ankles. Because Caroline wasn't thinking clearly and was distracted by the cold demeanor of the man in the suit, she didn't have a chance to fight or to jump overboard. She didn't notice the chains they were putting around her ankles with the weights until they were firmly attached. She tried to kick at the nearest man, but it was too late. Oh. My. God. She really was going to die. In one corner of her brain, she'd kept the hope alive she'd be able to escape, but it was obvious what they had in store for her.

The fancy-man was holding the camera again.

"Say goodbye to your SEAL, bitch. It didn't have to come to this. You could still tell me what I want to know." He paused as if giving her a chance to talk and to save her life.

Caroline glared at him, refusing to talk. She knew even if she spilled her guts now, he'd still kill her. He was crazy. He looked sane in his pressed and flawless suit, but it was obvious he was the craziest one of the bunch. Caroline didn't want to die, but at this point she didn't think she had any other option.

"That's what I thought. Brave to the end aren't you? Well, we'll see how brave you are when you're sitting on the bottom of the ocean. Oh don't worry, I'll make sure your SEAL sees your last minutes alive. I'm sure he'll blame himself for the rest of his life." He chuckled under his breath, laughing at himself. Then he nodded at the smelly man. He grabbed her under her arms and one of the other men grabbed her legs. The third man picked up the weights. They moved in tandem toward the side of the boat.

Caroline thrashed and fought against their hold. She raked her nails down the side of the closest man's face in desperation. She finally found her voice and started screaming. She pleaded with them not to do it and promised she'd tell them whatever they wanted to know. At the realization that her death was imminent all thoughts of being noble and brave flew out of her head. The men just laughed at her feeble attempts to get away and threw her over the side of the boat like they were throwing out the garbage.

Caroline gasped and tensed, knowing hitting the water was going to hurt...badly. She choked and sucked in a bunch of water when she hit. Damn, it *did* hurt; she landed on her side with the broken ribs. She felt herself sinking quickly. They hadn't tied her hands, so luckily she could use them to try to help get to the surface. Luckily, she was naturally buoyant. She'd never regret those extra fifteen pounds again.

She took a gasp of air before sinking downward again. She tried again and managed to tread water quickly enough to keep from sinking. The weights they'd tied to her ankles fortunately weren't too heavy. They'd underestimated her. She knew she wouldn't have the energy to keep it up for long though. She was heavy, in pain, and tired, and while she was a good swimmer, she knew she couldn't keep herself above water indefinitely. There was no way she'd survive if they left her in the middle of the ocean.

The waves were crashing over her head as she bobbed up and down. Caroline didn't know why she thought the water would be calm out in the middle of the ocean. It was a good thing she was a chemist and not an oceanographer. She swallowed water each time she took a gasping breath, but since she was getting some air, she didn't think she could complain.

She heard the fancy man call out from the boat. It was keeping near her, but not near enough for her to grab the side. They circled her, as if taunting her further.

"We'll pull you back in if you tell me about the plane. All you have to do is tell me how you knew about the ice and you'll live."

He was screwing with her and she knew it. She'd promised to tell them everything she knew before they threw her overboard. If he'd really wanted to know, he would've made the guys put her down and listened to her.

"Screw you!" Caroline cried out at the man, even though it wasn't much of a yell. She watched as the stupid red light on the camera kept blinking. The bastard was still filming her. The man next to him raised his arm. Oh geez. Really? Now they were going to shoot her? She choked back a sob. This would be so much easier if she didn't want to live so badly.

Caroline took a deep breath and let herself sink. She'd be damned if she'd be shot on top of everything else she'd gone through. Hijacked, stabbed, stalked, blown up, kidnapped, beaten, thrown overboard, and *then* shot? No. Just frickin' no.

She vaguely remembered a television show where the hosts proved that ducking underwater would protect a person from a bullet because once the bullet hit the water it slowed down or was deflected or something. She couldn't really remember the science behind it, but she hoped they hadn't made it all up.

She sank quickly. The weights around her ankles helped. Caroline stopped thinking and just sank. It was almost like floating. The silence was heavenly.

ABE FLOORED THEIR boat and headed straight at the other boat, now bobbing in the water. They'd watched in horror as Caroline was thrown overboard, screaming, then in relief when she came back up. It was now or never. Wolf and Benny were ready on board, Dude and Cookie were in their wet water gear and ready to go overboard. They'd discussed the plan and each of them knew their role. They'd worked together so long they could almost read each other's minds. They were a SEAL team, and they were here to do their job. Failure wasn't an option. It *definitely* wasn't an option when one of their own was involved. And Ice was theirs. One hundred percent.

They heard the shots as they pulled up near the terrorist's boat. Wolf's heart was in his throat. Caroline had to be okay, she just had to.

"Put down your weapons, United States Navy," Abe hollered through the loudspeaker of the boat. He aimed the floodlight at the other boat, partially blinding them. They saw two men hurry into the relative safety of the wheelhouse. At least the gunshots stopped with their actions. One of the men who'd run into the pilot house had been the one who'd been shooting at Caroline. The man in the suit just laughed and turned the handheld camera to them. The fourth man, the one who'd been on the video beating Caroline the most, just stood there arrogantly.

"You think you'll save her?" The suited man yelled. "I don't think so. Didn't you see the chains that were attached to her ankles? You'll never find her now. The bitch is on the bottom."

Keep him talking, keep him talking, Wolf said to himself over and over, refusing to rise to the bait of the other man. He had to distract him. He had to do his job. Caroline's life depended on it.

"Give yourself up now and you'll be spared." He responded loudly, knowing it wasn't going to happen, but he tried to convince the man anyway.

The man finally put down the camera.

"No way in hell!" He yelled back and pulled a pistol from his pants. He pointed it at the SEAL's ship and fired. Wolf ducked just in time and swore he heard the bullet pass over his head.

"I'll give you one more chance, asshole," Wolf yelled again, making sure to stay low in the boat.

When there was no answer, Benny gave Abe the signal to pull back from the terrorist's boat. They'd have to do this another way. They always had a Plan B. In fact most of the time Plan B was really Plan A, everyone knew it, but they'd always tried to go the "nice" route first.

Wolf knew the commander would be pissed, but they had other things to be concerned about, namely Caroline. They'd given the traitor a chance to give up, but he hadn't. They'd wanted to interrogate him, find out more about his connections and how ingrained the terrorist cell was, but now they had no choice. Everyone on the team hoped this was a fed working independently, but until they got back to base and analyzed the videotape of what was going on tonight, they'd never know.

It was standard operating procedure to film their missions when possible. Benny had hooked up the camera before they'd left the dock. Tex would be able to check it out and they'd see just how deep the traitor's reach had gone. Hell, Tex probably already knew who the traitor was by analyzing the security tapes at the marina. The man was spooky good at what he did.

There wasn't a lot of time to save Caroline and deal

with these assholes. It was them or Caroline, It wasn't even a choice. It was time to make their move.

Making the terrorists think they were giving up, the SEALs backed off. One of the men on the terrorist boat started its engine and began to peel away. Wolf and Abe could just hear his cackled laughter before he put the boat into full throttle. Counting down three seconds, Wolf turned his head to protect his eyes just as the boat exploded.

Pieces of the terrorist's boat rained down in the water around them. Wolf and Abe knew the terrorists wouldn't be an issue anymore.

Wolf didn't spare a second's thought for the four men who'd literally just exploded in front of his eyes. He didn't give a rat's ass about them. All he cared about was Caroline. Had they taken too long? Was she still alive?

CAROLINE FELT HERSELF sinking further and further down in the water. Her ears popped and it brought her out of her stupor. Shit, she'd sunk too far. She didn't think she was going to make it back to the surface before she ran out of air...or energy.

She hurt all over, but she had to try. She'd started to use her arms to swim back up to the surface when someone grabbed her from behind. Caroline panicked.

She kicked out with her bound legs, she tried to get her arms to move to hit whoever it was, but her arms were pinned to her sides. Oh Jesus, she was gonna die. She was going to die right here, after all she'd been through, after all her fighting and struggling. It wasn't fair. She might as well inhale as much water as she could to try to make it quick.

Caroline felt something being put over her face and tried to get away from whoever held her, but she couldn't fight her body's natural reaction of inhaling for the need of oxygen. This was it, she was dead....but somehow she wasn't.

She inhaled again. Oxygen. It was a diving mask over her face. She sucked in the oxygen greedily. She was still terrified, but at least for now, she had air. She tried to turn her head, but the hand holding the mask over her face was too strong. She started to panic again. Was she being kidnapped by the terrorists again? Had they laid in wait in the water making her think she was going to die before they caught her again? Was this some new kind of torture?

Just before a full-blown panic could set in, Caroline felt the person behind her take one of her hands in his and press his second and fourth fingers down hard. Caroline almost sobbed in relief. Matthew....no, it wasn't Matthew, but it was one of his team. She grabbed the man's hand and squeezed it has hard as she could, which probably wasn't really very hard in her condition, to let him know she understood. That she knew he was with Matthew. She was just so glad they'd found her. She wanted to cry, but she had to concentrate on breathing.

She had no idea how whoever it was behind her had ended up in the water with her just when she needed him, but she couldn't think about it now. She'd appreciate it later. She tried to relax. She went limp in the man's arms so he'd know for sure she understood he was there to help her.

He lifted one of her hands to the mask on her face and pressed hard. She nodded. She got it; she had to hold the mask on. She could do that.

Cookie relaxed a little. She'd understood. He was afraid Caroline would've been too far gone in her panic and pain and wouldn't remember what Wolf had told her about the signal to let her know who he was. After everything he'd heard about her from Wolf, Abe, and Mozart, he should've known she'd keep her head and trust him to do what he needed to do to make sure they both made it out alive.

Cookie had been prepared to knock her out if he had to, but it was so much easier with her cooperating with him. He was doubly thankful he'd gotten to her before she'd gone unconscious. It would've been much harder if he had to worry about doing CPR under water.

It wasn't something any of them wanted to have to do, but they'd been trained on the lifesaving technique. Cookie wasn't sure what was going on above their heads, but knew he was working on limited time.

Cookie couldn't do anything about the weight around Caroline's ankles right now, but the extra weight and the fact she couldn't use her legs wouldn't slow him down. He kicked away from the terrorist's boat. He had to get them moved a good distance before Dude blew it up. The shockwave under the water could kill them as easily as a bullet or inhaling water would.

He kicked hard; checking every now and then to make sure Ice was still holding the mask to her face and breathing the lifesaving oxygen.

Every time he looked down at her she was still breathing. He knew she'd had a close call. Even now he could tell she was using all her remaining energy to hold the mask on her face. She wasn't trying to help him swim. She was deadweight in his arms.

WOLF LOOKED AROUND. It was hard to see anything with all the parts of the exploded boat floating around them. Where was Dude? Where was Cookie? Where was Caroline? Fuck. He'd never been this anxious about the outcome of a mission before. Benny joined him at the side of the boat while Abe maneuvered slowly around the main wreckage site. They all scanned the surface for a glimpse of their teammates. Abe saw the signal first. It was Dude. He eased the boat over next to the man and Wolf and Benny helped pull him on board.

Dude pulled off his mask.

"Have you picked them up yet?" he asked, just as anxious as Wolf was. Wolf shook his head, knowing Dude meant Ice and Cookie then stood back up to scan the surface of the water again. Dude stood up and joined him.

"Cookie and I split up about two hundred feet from the boat. He went after Ice who'd ducked underwater right before that asshole shot at her. I went around to the front of the boat. Just as we planned, while you guys distracted them, I put the explosives on the bow and backed off just as they gunned it to leave. You know the rest."

Wolf nodded absently. He knew what the plan was and recognized Dude's part in the plan went off exactly as planned. Even with his busted up hand and missing fingers, Dude was the best demolition expert he'd ever seen. There wasn't a bomb around today he couldn't figure out how to disarm and there wasn't a type of explosive he couldn't use to its best advantage. Even with the thoughts running through his mind about how grateful to Dude he was for ending the standoff, he wondered where Cookie and Caroline were. He desperately needed to know she was okay and alive.

As Cookie swam Ice away from the boat she'd been thrown off of, he felt the explosion. It was close, but not too close. They'd made it. He continued swimming underwater to make sure they were safe from any flying debris. After everything she'd been through, Cookie didn't want them to be hit by anything either above or under the water. He swam a bit further than what he figured was safe just to make sure they were in the clear and cloaked by darkness. He didn't know exactly what had gone down above their heads…he knew what was *supposed* to have happened, but he also knew that wasn't always what *did* happen.

After judging they'd gone far enough, Cookie eased them slowly toward the surface. It was pitch dark now. He saw the SEAL boat about five hundred yards off to his left, its lights bobbing up and down in the waves, but didn't immediately signal. He had to make sure it really was safe and that Ice was all right. He knew Wolf would be pissed at the delay, but he wasn't going to risk Ice's life after everything she'd been though.

He still held her firmly with one arm. She was heavy from the chain around her ankles, but she wasn't in danger of sinking. Cookie was the best swimmer of all of them. That was part of the reason he was chosen to be in the water in the first place. Wolf had volunteered to go, but they all knew he had to be on the boat. The man on the tape knew who he was and it'd be better if he was there to try to negotiate with him. Cookie knew it killed Wolf to back off and agree. Unspoken was the fact that if Caroline hadn't survived whatever the terrorists had done to her, Wolf would lose it. It was better to have Cookie in the water, just in case.

Cookie held Ice's back to his front with one arm, and tried to ease her hands down from the mask with the other. She was still holding it in place with a death grip.

Caroline repeated to herself, *Don't let go. Don't let go. Don't let go.* It was her mantra. She was so tired and hurt so much, but she knew she had to keep holding that mask to her face, otherwise she'd die. Caroline heard something…she tried to concentrate, but she was so tired…finally she realized it was someone talking to her.

"It's okay, Ice, you're okay. You can let go of the mask now, you're all right. You made it. I've got you. We're not underwater anymore…you're safe…" Cookie kept talking to her soothingly. He'd keep it up as long as it took for her to come out of her stupor.

Caroline opened her swollen eyes as far as they'd go. She couldn't see much, as it was dark, but she could see a light bobbing off in the distance. She could feel herself bobbing up and down in the waves. She tried to relax her arms, but they wouldn't move. Finally she forced her screaming muscles to let go of the mask. Cookie reached up and removed the mask from her face as soon as she let go, and Caroline took a shallow breath, any more deeply hurt her ribs. She grabbed on to the arm that was across her chest holding her up. She couldn't see the man behind her, but she knew he was one of the good guys; he was one of Matthew's teammates.

"Th-th-thank you," she got out in a low cracked voice.

Cookie squeezed her chest gently in response. "You did all the hard work, Ice. I was just there at the end when you needed a little help. How about we get out of here?" he asked softly. He felt her nod and smiled. He activated the signal light and waited.

"LOOK!" BENNY SAID while pointing off into the distance. They all looked and saw a light bobbing in the water about five hundred yards away.

"Thank God," Wolf muttered, knowing that Cookie would have found Caroline. He refused to think differently. He turned to make sure Abe had seen Cookie, but Abe was already turning the boat and heading in their direction. Wolf watched as the light got closer and closer. Finally he could see Caroline safe in

Cookie's arms. He thought he'd lost her for good. God. When they didn't immediately find either her or Cookie, Wolf had begun to think the worst. He should've known she was too stubborn to die. Abe pulled the boat up next to them.

"Careful, Wolf," Cookie said softly. "She's hurt pretty badly. She also has that chain around her ankles."

Wolf clenched his fists. He wanted to go back and kill the men again. He nodded stiffly signaling he'd heard his buddy's words.

Cookie leaned in close to Caroline again.

"Ice, you have to let go of my arm. Wolf is here...he'll help you on the boat...okay?"

Caroline nodded and opened her puffy swollen eyes again but shut them quickly. The light from the boat hurt her eyes. She cautiously uncurled her fingers from around Cookie's arm and waited.

She couldn't help herself. She just waited for some-one to haul her butt on the boat. Finally she felt Matthew's arms go around her waist and felt Cookie let go. She felt really heavy...oh yeah, she still had the weights around her ankles.

Wolf gingerly took Caroline by the waist and grasped her to him. She was heavy, and he saw it was because of the chain and weight around her ankles. He eased her over the side of the boat and when he saw she'd cleared it, he lay backward on the deck with

Caroline on top of him. The water from her clothes quickly soaked him, but he didn't even notice. Her arms hadn't reached around him, but stayed clenched together in front of her, against his chest. He could hear her shallow breathing.

"My God, Caroline," he whispered to her. "Thank God. Thank God. I've got you. You're safe." He was babbling and couldn't stop. All he knew was that his Caroline was in his arms, battered and bruised, but safe.

Caroline heard Matthew in the recesses of her mind. She somehow found the strength to open her eyes to slits. She couldn't lift her head from the crease of his neck, but she managed to unfurl one fist and lay it flat on his chest. She could feel his heart beating under her hand, and it calmed her. She was finally safe. "I'm getting you all wet," she said softly, then promptly passed out.

Benny and Dude cut the chain off her ankles as they headed back to shore. Wolf didn't move. He couldn't. He wrapped his arms around his woman and held on tight. He could see her swollen eyes and saw that blood was still oozing from her head somewhere. She'd been through hell, but she was here, and alive.

Cookie covered Ice and Wolf with a blanket. Wolf nodded his head in thanks at his teammate. He held Caroline close to his chest and prayed she'd be okay. He counted her breaths, taking solace in the fact that she was actually breathing after everything she'd been through. She felt so fragile in his arms. He was scared to move her. He knew she was hurt. This happened to her because of him. He knew she wouldn't agree, but he knew the truth. He had some decisions to make.

Chapter Eighteen

CAROLINE GROANED. SHE hurt. She tried to remember what she'd done that had made her so sore. It came back to her in a flash. The cabin, Matthew, the warehouse, the boat...she opened her eyes, or at least tried to. Wow, her face hurt. She reached a hand up to her face and felt how swollen it was. Oh man. Finally she got her eyes open a crack and looked around. A hospital room. She was in the hospital. She *hated* hospitals. She looked around. It was empty except for her. She tried to push down the disappointment she felt. Matthew had no reason to be there when she woke up, but she'd hoped he would be anyway. Where was everyone? She wanted out of there...she wanted...hell. She closed her eyes and was asleep again in seconds.

AFTER DROPPING CAROLINE off at the Navy hospital, Wolf and his team called their commander. They'd explained all that had happened that night. Tex had analyzed the tapes and enhanced them. Surprisingly, the man in the suit was easy to identify. When Tex had sent the picture to Wolf, he'd recognized the man immediately.

He was an FBI agent, and they'd actually talked to him in Nebraska after they'd landed the plane. It was no wonder he'd been close enough to be able to come and talk to them. He'd arranged for the plane to crash in the first place. He'd obviously volunteered to come to Nebraska and interview them. Wolf, Abe, and Mozart had felt something was off about the interrogator after they'd been interviewed. Their instincts were dead on.

They had no idea what his real motives were behind his double-cross, but at this point it didn't really matter. The only thing that mattered to Wolf was that they'd rescued Caroline. It was up to the rest of the Feds to see how deep his betrayal went. For the country's sake, Wolf hoped he was working alone. God only knew their job was hard enough without having to constantly battle domestic terrorists as well as foreign ones.

Wolf was thankful they'd kept what had really happened close to their chests. The only person they'd told all the details about the flight and Caroline's role in it had been their own SEAL commander. They'd have to report all that had happened in Virginia, and the repercussions would be long lasting most likely, both for the FBI and the SEAL team, but Wolf couldn't bring himself to regret it. Not as long as Caroline was safe.

WOLF TRIED TO ignore his teammates. They weren't happy with him. Not happy was an understatement, they were pissed. They'd argued most of the night and he still wasn't swayed. He was no good for Caroline. Look what had happened to her after she met him. Nothing but bad things. She'd almost died in a plane hijacking, her apartment had been broken into, she was put in the witness protection program, she'd been kidnapped, beaten up, shot at, and then almost drowned. It wasn't safe for any SEAL to be in a relationship. Why couldn't his team members see that?

They'd wanted to wait for Ice to wake up when they'd brought her into the hospital. Cookie, Benny, and Dude needed to meet her while she was conscious, not half conscious on the bottom of a boat. Cookie more than the others. Caroline seemed to affect everyone the same way. She impressed the hell out of Cookie, and that was a hard thing to do. He told them all how she'd panicked, but recognized their signal to her right away. How she relaxed and let Cookie swim them to safety, and even how she'd thanked him while floating in the middle of the damn ocean.

They were pissed Wolf was seemingly giving up on her. They couldn't understand how Wolf could just leave Ice to recuperate alone in the hospital after all of his angst about rescuing her. They *knew* he loved her, but for some reason he was being stubborn now that she was safe.

Wolf could only think about all that Caroline had been through. She had two broken ribs and too many cuts, bruises, and scrapes to count. Her wrists were heavily bandaged and she'd received eight stitches in a cut on her head. She was dehydrated and weak from not eating or drinking anything. She'd taken a hell of a beating and still had her wits about her. When she was delirious in the boat and on the way to the hospital she kept repeating, "I didn't talk, I swear I didn't tell him anything," over and over. Wolf had been able to reassure her, but as soon as he let go of her and placed her on the gurney in the hospital, she started saying it again. It literally broke his heart to leave her there, but he *knew* it was the right thing to do, no matter what his team said.

COOKIE, BENNY, AND DUDE tiptoed into the hospital room, as much as three grown men could tiptoe. They went over to the woman lying in the hospital bed by the window. She was sleeping. She looked horrible. Her face was covered in bruises, her arms weren't much better. They couldn't see the rest of her, but they knew she had a couple of broken ribs and was most likely covered in bruises everywhere else as well.

The three men had wanted to stay with her when she was brought in, but Wolf refused to let them. They'd come today without him knowing. They had to meet her in person. They'd heard so much about her from Mozart and Abe, and even watching Wolf with her on the boat.

Women weren't something they'd ever given much thought to in the past. They loved women, loved *sleeping* with women, but had never thought much about them beyond that. They wondered why this woman was so special, what was it about her that made their teammates do things they never would've done before meeting her? Cookie and Benny sat on one side of her and Dude sat on the other.

Caroline stirred, restless. What had woken her up? She opened her eyes and kept herself from shrieking, barely. There were three men sitting around her bed. Big men. Were they there to harm her? Had Wolf captured all the terrorists? She tried to think…did she have any weapons? Just before she went into a full blown panic one of the men held out his hand to her.

"Nice to meet you Ice, I'm Dude."

Caroline looked at the man and his outstretched hand. Dude. One of Matthew's men? She reached out and grasped his hand in hers cautiously and shook his hand. She decided to give him the benefit of the doubt.

"Nice to meet you, I'm Caroline." Her voice came out scratchy and low.

She waited, and finally felt it. His second and fourth fingers pressed harder than the rest of his hand against hers. She smiled. "Faulkner, right?" Caroline asked the big man.

He nodded and smiled, but said, "Dude."

"I'm Benny," another one of the men said to her softly. Caroline turned toward him to shake his hand and received the same signal from him. They were Matthew's teammates. Thank God. She didn't think she had it in her at the moment to escape another damn terrorist.

"Benny…" she thought for a moment then tentatively said, "Kason?"

Benny brought her hand up to his lips and kissed it gently. "That's me."

Caroline turned to the third man as Kason let go of her hand. "And you have to be Hunter," She said shakily, feeling emotionally raw at meeting the man who'd literally held her life in his arms.

He nodded and instead of holding out his hand to her he stood up and leaned over. He gathered her carefully into his arms and into a tight comforting hug. It felt right to Caroline. It still hurt a little bit, but she ignored the pain and concentrated on showing her appreciation to the big SEAL holding her.

"Thank you, Hunter," she said earnestly in his ear. "Thank you." She didn't have to say anything else. She felt Hunter nod and then carefully, he laid her back down on the bed.

Caroline looked at the three men sitting around her.

"It's so good to finally meet you guys. Are you all okay? I'm not sure what happened out there. I know Hunter saved me when I was under the water, but I only have flashes here and there of what went on after that. What happened to the fancy-man?"

Dude knew who she was talking about and could hear the fear in her voice. "It's over, Ice. You don't have to worry about him ever again. He was the man behind everything. He was a disgruntled FBI agent. It looks like he was working on his own and didn't have an entire network or anything. He can't send anyone else after you. You're safe." Dude wasn't one hundred percent certain that was true, but there was no way in hell he'd say anything to worry Ice in any way. She'd been through enough.

Caroline let out a breath of relief. "Thank God. But are you guys okay? Everyone else is all right?"

Benny nodded. "We're all fine Ice. It's *you* we're concerned about."

Caroline tried not to cry. It was nice to be worried about, but if she was honest with herself, these weren't the men she really wanted to see. She wanted to see

Matthew, to make sure he was okay…hell, to just be with him. But he hadn't been by at all. She hadn't seen him since the boat, and she hardly remembered much of that. It was obvious he'd decided she wasn't worth it. It hurt. She'd thought he really liked her. He was damn good at acting that was for sure.

"How's Sam?" Caroline asked quickly, trying to hide her pain that Matthew didn't want to see her.

"He's good." Cookie told her. "Bitching to get out of the hospital and back to work. He'll be coming back to San Diego with us in the next few days." He didn't mention the scarring on Mozart's face and how bad it was. Cookie knew Caroline probably felt bad enough as it was.

Caroline's heart sunk after hearing Hunter's words. So they were leaving. Soon. In the next few days. She knew they would be, but she'd hoped to see Matthew, or at least talk to him before they left. She tried to pull herself together.

"I'm sure he is," she said with a forced laugh. "Tell him I said hello?"

"Of course, Ice. He'd be here if he could." Benny told her.

"I know. I'm just glad he's okay."

There was a moment of silence in the room. Caroline didn't want to ask where Matthew was, or why he hadn't come to see her. But she *so* wanted to know. As if he could read her mind Cookie told her gently, "He doesn't know we're here."

Caroline nodded, even though it felt like her heart was being ripped out. Matthew didn't want to see her and didn't want his friends seeing her. That hurt more than she'd ever admit to anyone.

Benny continued, trying to make her feel better, "We wanted to meet you...*really* meet you. It's weird not knowing one of our own teammates." He smiled at her.

Caroline tried to smile back, but figured she'd failed miserably when Kason didn't smile back at her. "Thanks guys, but you know I'm not a part of the team. I just got in the way of *your* team."

Not one of the three men cracked a smile.

Cookie reached into his pocket and pulled something out. He took one of her hands, placed whatever it was in her palm, and gently closed her hand around it before she could see what it was. When he sat back without a word, Caroline opened her hand and looked down. It was his SEAL trident pin.

"You *are* a part of this team, Ice." He told her. "I can't think of any other person, male or female, that would've been as tough as you've been these last few weeks. You didn't break, you didn't hesitate to do what you thought was right, even when you were scared. Most importantly you've saved our teammates lives…more than once. If you need us, all you have to do is ask."

He put one finger under Caroline's chin and lifted her eyes up to his and put his hand over hers as she gripped the pin tightly. "I don't know if you know anything about The Budweiser pin and what it symbolizes." When she shook her head, Cookie continued. "Every SEAL gets their pin after they've finished BUD/S training, completed SEAL Qualification Training, and can officially call themselves a SEAL. It symbolizes that we are brothers in arms that we train together and fight together. It's the one thing most of us are most proud of."

"But…" Caroline tried to interject, but Cookie spoke over her.

"You're one of us. You earned your Budweiser pin, Ice. You *more* than earned it."

Caroline felt a tear slip from her swollen eye and her lip quiver. All she could do was nod. She was so touched by Cookie's gesture. She wanted to throw her arms around him, but she knew it'd hurt too much. She probably should say something profound, but she just had one thought running through her mind. She knew the guys would help her.

"Can you get me out of here?" She pleaded softly, choking back a sob, "I hate hospitals."

ABE SAT DOWN next to Wolf. He wanted to beat the hell out of his friend, but decided to try to talk some sense into him instead.

"I talked to Mozart yesterday," he said quietly.

Wolf nodded. Mozart was okay. He'd finally woken up and seemed to be all right. His face would always be scarred and it'd still be quite a while before it healed, but overall he'd been lucky. He'd be joining the team again when they got back to San Diego.

"We talked about what happened at the cabin." Wolf winced. He didn't remember any of it. He only remembered the fire and trying to breathe, and then nothing else. Since the only people that had been there were Caroline and Mozart, he hadn't known what had happened to get Caroline kidnapped, except that he hadn't protected her. He hadn't done his job. He was having a hard time getting over the guilt of that.

Abe gave his team leader a quick rundown of what Mozart had told him went on when he arrived.

"After Mozart shot the two terrorists waiting at the window to kill anyone that came out, he saw Ice. He tried to get her out, but she wouldn't leave without you. She dragged you to the window and made Mozart get you out first. He asked her what the hell she was thinking and she told him that SEALs don't leave SEALs behind."

Abe let Wolf absorb that, then continued. "She was

in a house that was burning down around her. Instead of getting out as fast as she could, she made sure *you* got out first. She wouldn't leave you. She fought as hard as she could, and when she realized the only way to protect you was to go with that asshole willingly...she did."

Abe watched his team leader struggling with the truth of Caroline's actions for a moment.

"The way I see it Wolf, is that if she wouldn't leave you behind in a fucking burning building...why are you leaving her behind now? You *know* she doesn't like hospitals. Remember when we tried to make her see a doctor after she got hurt on the plane? Remember how she'd reacted? Jesus, Wolf, we all know you two are crazy about each other. We know she's yours. Why are you doing this to Caroline and to yourself?"

"She's in there because of me," Wolf admitted out loud for the first time.

"Bullshit," Abe said immediately, surprising Wolf with his emphatic assessment.

"She's in there because she's one tough chick. Most women I know would've given up and died. Hell, most women I know would've cowered in the back of that plane and done nothing. Think about it. If I *ever* find a woman who puts me first, who looks out for me before she looks out for herself, I'm grabbing her and never letting go. If Ice wasn't as tough as she was, she would've died five different ways. But she didn't. She's still alive and wishing you were there with her. You have one hell of a woman, and you're throwing her away. She's loyal as hell and doesn't take any shit from anyone. Just the kind of woman you need. You'll never find another like her. She's yours. You just have to be brave enough to go and take what you want for once in your damn life. There's no guarantee any of us will be around tomorrow. We could fall down a flight of stairs or be hit by a car walking across a street. There are no guarantees in life, but I can guaran-damn-tee if you don't go to her now, you *will* regret it the rest of your life."

Abe waited and let that sink in. Then he continued. "Benny, Dude, and Cookie went to meet her yesterday."

At that, Wolf looked up quickly. He didn't want to ask, but then again he didn't have to. Abe knew what he wanted to know.

"She looks like hell. She's beaten up and depressed. Cookie gave her his Budweiser pin. Said she was a part of this team."

Wolf clenched his teeth. *He* wanted to be the one with her. *He* wanted to be the one welcoming her to the team with his pin. But he couldn't. It was the only way he could think of to protect her.

"She asked a favor of them," Abe told him. "She wanted their help in getting her out of the hospital."

"She's not ready to be released!" Wolf burst out furiously. "What the hell is she thinking? Tell me they didn't!"

Abe continued calmly, ignoring Wolf's outburst. "Did she ever tell you why she didn't like hospitals?"

Wolf shook his head, remembering back to when Mozart had stitched her up in the plane, she'd told them she didn't like hospitals.

"While you've had your head up your ass, I've had Tex do some digging for me." Abe told him testily. "When she was twenty two she was in a car accident. She spent three months in traction in the hospital. Her parents couldn't come to her because her dad had just started a new job and wasn't able to take any leave. They were older, and her mom didn't feel comfortable traveling by herself. Besides, Ice told her she was fine. Unsurprisingly, she downplayed her injuries to her mom. Apparently she had a lot of complications, but the hospital was overcrowded and busy. She had *two* visitors the entire time she was there. One was the lawyer of the guy that hit her, and the other was a man she'd been dating. He came once, and never returned. She sat in that room day and night and suffered through bed sores and other 'minor' ailments because no one was there to fight for her. No one cared about the single, ordinary woman sitting alone in her room day after day." Abe fell silent, letting what he'd said sink in.

Wolf clenched his teeth hard. No wonder his Caroline was so strong. She had to be.

Abe could see Wolf was hurting. He hadn't meant to upset him, but he had to make him see what he was throwing away.

"The guys sprung her from the hospital and took her back to her apartment. She told them she'd be fine, and they left. Then they came to see me." He paused. "A SEAL doesn't leave a SEAL behind. Ever, Wolf. Would you really leave her behind and go back to San Diego thinking that she means nothing to you? Would you really leave here letting *her* think she was a burden to you...to us? Because that's what she thinks. She thinks the same thing that you do, that it's *her* fault we were even involved in anything that happened. I *can* tell you this; if you don't want her, that's fine, but know that the rest of the team will be keeping in touch with her. We like her. We respect her. We'll take care of her if you don't."

"Don't *want* her Abe?" Wolf said incredulously, not able to stand the harangue anymore. He stood up abruptly and paced the room. "God there's nothing I want more. But..."

Abe interrupted him. "But nothing, Wolf. If you want her, you'd better go and get her. Otherwise she'll find someone else."

Abe clasped Wolf on the shoulder in the way that men did, and walked away. He'd said what he had to say. If Wolf didn't listen to him, he'd request a transfer to another team. He couldn't work for a man who wouldn't do what was best for himself and the woman he loved.

Ten minutes later Abe watched as Wolf left the building and got into a rental car. He sure hoped Wolf was going to get his woman. Abe had done everything he could; it was up to Wolf now.

CAROLINE HEARD THE ringing of her doorbell, but she ignored it. She snuggled down deeper into the couch. She didn't want to see anyone. She didn't want to talk to anyone. She'd even put off calling her boss. She had no idea if she still had a job or not, but she didn't feel good enough to deal with anyone yet. All she wanted to do was close her eyes and forget the last few weeks ever happened, well most of it at least.

When the ringing of her front door bell didn't stop, Caroline drew the blanket up over her head gingerly. She figured it was probably someone trying to sell her something, because she couldn't imagine who else would be at her door. Hell, she didn't *know* anyone other than the SEAL team, and she'd sent Hunter, Kason, and Faulkner away the day before firmly. She told them she was fine, felt great, and that she'd keep in touch with them.

The fact was she wasn't okay. She was depressed and

still in quite a bit of pain. She wasn't hungry and hadn't bothered to get dressed. Finally the ringing of her doorbell stopped. Thank God. She closed her eyes, maybe if she slept long enough, the pain, both emotional and physical, would go away.

Wolf made quick work of the lock on Caroline's door. She really needed to get better security. Anyone who knew anything about picking locks, like him, could get in. No wonder the damn terrorist had been able to get in so easily. He closed the door softly behind him and walked into Caroline's apartment. Everything was quiet. He walked through her kitchen into the living room and saw Caroline bundled up on the couch. The blanket covered her from head to toe; all he could see was the top of her head. He went over and kneeled down next to her.

"Caroline," he said softly.

Caroline wasn't quite asleep when she heard her name. She opened her eyes and sat up quickly. She saw Matthew as the blanket slid off her face, then groaned and fell back onto the couch. Damn. That hurt.

"I'm so sorry sweetheart," Wolf fretted, "I didn't mean to scare you."

"How'd you get in here? Oh, never mind," Caroline whined petulantly. He was a SEAL; a locked door wouldn't keep him out. "What do you want?"

"You," Wolf said simply. He was sick of beating

around the bush with this woman.

Caroline opened her eyes and looked at the man kneeling next to her. "What?" She questioned, not believing what she'd heard.

"You. I want you." Wolf repeated. "I've been an idiot. Every day since I left you in that hospital I've been kicking myself and wanting to get back to you. I'm not the most romantic guy you'll ever meet, but you won't meet one more devoted to you. I'm sorry I was a jerk, but I'm here now and I don't want to let you go."

Caroline lay there stunned. Matthew was saying everything she'd ever wanted a man to say, but was he serious? Of course he was. He wouldn't have said it if he wasn't.

"I thought you'd left," she murmured sadly, looking Matthew in his eyes.

"I couldn't," Wolf told her honestly. He stood up and gathered Caroline carefully in his arms, sat on the couch, and settled her onto his lap. He rejoiced when she didn't complain, but instead curled up into his chest and shut her eyes.

Caroline thought he smelled so good and she was so tired.

"It's okay, go ahead and sleep, baby, I'm not going anywhere."

Caroline realized she must've said that last bit out loud about being tired. She nodded and was out within seconds.

Wolf sat with Caroline on his lap for about an hour just watching her sleep and stroking her hair. He was so thankful she hadn't thrown him out yet, but he also knew she was exhausted and probably not thinking straight. Finally he laid her back on the couch carefully, brushed his finger down her still healing face, took off his jacket, and went into the kitchen to get to work.

When Caroline woke up she smelled something delicious. She sat up slowly and groaned. Jesus, she was sick of feeling helpless. Suddenly Matthew was there, he was actually still there.

"You need to eat Caroline," he told her gently. "I've made you some soup."

"You're still here." The words popped out without her even thinking about them.

"I'm still here. Now, come on. Up you go." He helped her up and into the little dining area off the kitchen. He settled her into a chair and shook out two pain pills.

"I don't like taking those," Caroline told him petulantly.

"Doesn't matter," he retorted. "You need them, you're in pain."

"They make me drowsy and I feel weird when I take them," Caroline whined feeling grumpy and out of sorts.

"Ice. You need them. Please. I'll be here to help you, and you can sleep as long as you want to."

"What do you mean?" She asked him carefully.

"I mean I'm here for as long as you need me."

"Then what?" She asked Matthew sternly. "What about when I'm all better and don't need you here anymore?"

"I'm hoping you'll always need me as much as I need you."

Caroline sat in stunned silence. Her heart lightened a little bit. He *sounded* serious, but was he really?

Wolf continued as if his words hadn't just changed her life. "I know we'll have to work some things out with our jobs, but all I know is that I don't want to let you go. I want to spend all my time with you when I'm not working. I want to come home to you, and only you, after a mission. Please say you'll give us a chance."

Wolf stopped and waited. She held his heart in her hands.

A tear slipped down Caroline's face. "Yes, Matthew. I want that too. I'm scared. I know what you do is dangerous as hell. I don't want to lose you."

"You won't lose me. I won't allow it."

Caroline smiled. She had no idea how they'd make things work, but she knew she'd do whatever it took. She loved this man.

"I love you, Matthew." She suddenly realized she'd

never told him.

"I love you too, Caroline. And you'll give Cookie back his damn Trident. If you're going to keep anyone's Budweiser pin, it'll be mine."

Caroline smiled. She knew the pin was a big deal, but obviously she hadn't worked out in her head just *how* important it was. "Okay, Matthew," she told him contentedly. Caroline knew everything would all work out. Matthew would make sure of it.

Epilogue

"SERIOUSLY, HUNTER, QUIT it. I'm not an invalid. I can carry some of my stuff."

"I know you're not an invalid, Ice, but this box is too heavy for you. I got it."

Caroline huffed and let Hunter take the box out of her arms and watched as he carried it into the house. She really couldn't stay mad at any of Matthew's friends. She loved them all. Not as much as she loved Matthew, but she didn't know what she'd do without them. They'd done their best to make sure she and Matthew had time together while they'd been living on opposite sides of the country. She knew they'd taken some assignments for him and had let him take extra time off just so he could fly out to see her.

The first time she'd seen Sam's face she'd broken down in sobs. She hadn't been crying because of his looks, exactly. She'd told him flat out, "It's my fault."

Mozart had been pissed and had held her face in his hands and sternly said, "Bull. Ice, *you* didn't do this.

The terrorists did. If I had to do it again, I'd do it all exactly the same way."

"But your poor face..." Sam didn't say anything but just crossed his arms and glared at her.

Finally he put two fingers over her lips and wouldn't let her continue her thoughts. "Seriously, I'm all right. Yeah, I have scars. Yeah, women sometimes look over and through me as a result, but it doesn't mean a damn thing to me, Ice. Now I don't want to hear you ever apologize to me about it again. Hear me?"

Caroline could only nod. "Okay, but you *will* let me find some of that cream that can help reduce the scarring. I know some women get it when they have C-sections. You'll put it on every night until I tell you you're done with it." She tried to sound bossy, but didn't know how well she'd succeeded when Sam just laughed at her and brought her toward him with a hand at her neck and kissed her forehead.

Caroline had watched Sam after that, and it looked like he'd told her the truth. He didn't seem to care about his face, and as time went on it had healed somewhat, but he'd never be as "pretty" as he'd been before. She'd given him the tube of cream she'd threatened to get for him. He'd grumbled about it, but had promised he'd been using it. Caroline knew it'd never be enough to completely make the feelings of guilt subside, but she'd promised not to bring it up again.

After five months of dating, Caroline had had enough of her long distance relationship with Matthew. She told him while they were lying in bed one night that she didn't want to waste any more time. She'd contacted her old boss back in California and he'd agreed to let her have her old job back. They hadn't been able to find a replacement for her yet, so he was thrilled to have her back in the fold.

Matthew didn't waste any time. The second she said she wanted to move back to California, he'd contacted a real estate agent and gotten to work trying to find them a place to live. They'd finally agreed on a small house with a full basement. It wasn't her dream house, but she'd live anywhere as long as Matthew was with her.

They'd spent some hilarious nights with the team. Caroline thought, as she had the first time she'd seen them, they were sex-on-a-stick, and apparently the ladies in California did too. They all rotated girlfriends as often as she changed her shoes, which was a *lot*. Even Sam's scars didn't seem to deter many women, much to her relief. Caroline tolerated the skanky women as best she could. Luckily Matthew knew how she felt and when they all met up on date night, he'd excuse them early.

They'd go home and make love until the wee hours of the morning. That was one of the best things about being in the same town as Matthew. She could have him whenever she wanted. And she wanted him a lot. They were well matched as far as their libidos went. Matthew never seemed to get tired of her and always complimented her lavishly. In return she'd let Matthew get bossy in bed. But when he got bossy, she never went to sleep unsatisfied. It was a good tradeoff.

Caroline's life was wonderful and she couldn't be happier. She found it extremely nerve-racking whenever Matthew and his team had to head out on a mission, but one night, seeing her stressing about it, Matthew had tried to reassure her.

"Caroline, I know it's not easy to be with me, but you have to know I'll do whatever it takes to get back to you. How could I do anything less when you fought so hard to stay alive until I could find you and rescue you? Trust me. Trust in the team."

She'd understood. She *had* fought to live, for him. If she hadn't loved him she would've given up long before she found herself in the middle of the ocean struggling to stay afloat.

All was well in her life. She had almost everything she ever wanted. The only thing missing was girlfriends. She hadn't had any close friends in her life, but she wanted that. All around her she saw moms shopping with their daughters, friends at the spa enjoying the day, or women sitting down for a quick lunch during the work week.

She hoped Matthew's team would find women to love, women she could be friends with, but she was losing hope. The bitches the men hung out with were definitely *not* the kind of people she wanted to associate with. She had no idea what they saw in them...okay, well she *did*, but she knew none of them were good enough for them outside the bedroom.

Caroline thought about Christopher. He was dating one of the worst of the bunch, some chick named Adelaide. She acted like she was so much better than Caroline and it drove her crazy. She figured she must be *really* good in bed, because the Christopher *she* knew deserved so much better. She knew part of his past, and it was time he found a good woman. Someone who'd put him first. She sighed. She might as well wish for the moon. Adelaide knew she'd latched onto someone so much better than her. Who knew what she'd do to keep him?

Caroline felt arms come around her and pull her backward. She leaned back into Matthew.

"Happy?"

"You have to ask?" Caroline scolded him. She laid her head on his shoulder and felt him turn his head to kiss her temple.

"The house isn't too small for you?"

Caroline turned in Matthew's arms. "I couldn't care less where we live. I just want to fall asleep in your arms every night and wake up in them in the morning. I love you. I'd go thorough everything all over again as long as it meant I'd end up right here again."

Wolf didn't say anything, just leaned down and kissed her. Hard.

"Hey you two, quit it! Come help us carry more boxes in."

They laughed as Faulkner bitched at them. Caroline smiled up at Matthew. She had no idea how she'd been lucky enough to end up with this man, but she wasn't giving him back. He was hers. Now and forever.

Look for the next book in the
SEAL of Protection Series:
Protecting Alabama.

Discover other titles by Susan Stoker

SEAL of Protection Series

Protecting Caroline

Protecting Alabama

Protecting Fiona

Marrying Caroline (novella)

Protecting Summer

Protecting Cheyenne

Protecting Jessyka

Protecting Julie (novella)

Protecting Melody

Protecting the Future

Delta Force Heroes Series

Rescuing Rayne

Assisting Aimee (loosely related to DF)

Rescuing Emily

Rescuing Harley

Rescuing Kassie (TBA)

Rescuing Casey (TBA)

Rescuing Wendy (TBA)

Rescuing Mary (TBA)

Badge of Honor: Texas Heroes Series

Justice for Mackenzie
Justice for Mickie
Justice for Corrie
Justice for Laine (novella)
Shelter for Elizabeth
Justice for Boone
Shelter for Adeline (TBA)
Justice for Sidney (TBA)
Shelter for Blythe (TBA)
Justice for Milena (TBA)
Shelter for Sophie (TBA)
Justice for Kinley (TBA)
Shelter for Promise (TBA)
Shelter for Koren (TBA)
Shelter for Penelope (TBA)

Beyond Reality Series

Outback Hearts
Flaming Hearts
Frozen Hearts

Writing as Annie George

Stepbrother Virgin (erotic novella)

Connect with Susan Online

Susan's Facebook Profile and Page:
www.facebook.com/authorsstoker
www.facebook.com/authorsusanstoker

Follow Susan on Twitter:
www.twitter.com/Susan_Stoker

Find Susan's Books on Goodreads:
www.goodreads.com/SusanStoker

Email: Susan@StokerAces.com

Website: www.StokerAces.com

To sign up for Susan's Newsletter go to:
http://bit.ly/SusanStokerNewsletter

Or text: STOKER to 24587 for text alerts on your
mobile device

About the Author

New York Times, USA Today, and *Wall Street Journal* Bestselling Author Susan Stoker has a heart as big as the state of Texas, where she lives, but this all-American girl has also spent the last fourteen years living in Missouri, California, Colorado, and Indiana. She's married to a retired Army man who now gets to follow *her* around the country.

She debuted her first series in 2014 and quickly followed that up with the SEAL of Protection Series, which solidified her love of writing and creating stories readers can get lost in.

If you enjoyed this book, or any book, please consider leaving a review. It's appreciated by authors more than you'll know.